D0191517

The Kid and Me

A Novel

Frederick Turner

University of Nebraska Press | Lincoln and London

Library of Congress
Cataloging-in-Publication Data
Names: Turner, Frederick W., 1937–, author.
Title: The kid and me: a novel / Frederick Turner.
Description: Lincoln: University of
Nebraska Press, [2018]
Identifiers: LCCN 2017054273
ISBN 9781496206893 (softcover: alk. paper)
ISBN 9781496208125 (epub)
ISBN 9781496208132 (mobi)
ISBN 9781496208149 (pdf)
Subjects: LCSH: Lincoln County (N.M.)—
History—19th century—Fiction. | Frontier and
pioneer life—New Mexico—Fiction. | Billy, the
Kid,—Fiction. | Vendetta—Fiction. | BISAC:
FICTION / Westerns. | GSAFD: Western stories.
Classification: LCC PS3620.U765 K53 2018 |
DDC 813/.6—dc23 LC record available at
https://lccn.loc.gov/2017054273

Designed and set in Scala OT by L. Auten.

For Ronald

Characters

GEORGE COE .... Farmer, gunfighter, painter, roadside storyteller

THE FIRM .... Lincoln County commercial outfit run by L. G. Murphy, Jimmy Dolan, and others; backed by the Santa Fe Ring

TUNSTALL, MCSWEEN, CHISUM.......... Rival commercial outfit

BUCKSHOT ROBERTS
JESSE EVANS
KIP BROWN
WINN RIGNEY
BUCK MORTON
TOM HILL
FRANK BAKER
ANDY BOYLE

} Hired hands of the Firm

BILLY BONNEY, AKA KID
  ANTRIM, BILLY THE KID
TOM O'FOLLIARD
FRANK COE
HENDRY BROWN
CHARLIE BOWDRE
FRANK MCNABB
FRED WAITE
DOC SCURLOCK
JOHN MIDDLETON
DICK BREWER
JIM FRENCH

} Hired hands of Tunstall, McSween, Chisum

WILLIAM BRADY
DAD PEPPIN
GEORGE HINDMAN
BILLY MATTHEWS
} Town of Lincoln lawmen

PAT GARRETT . . . . Sheriff, deputy U. S. marshal, Lincoln County

TOM CATRON . . . . Boss, Santa Fe Ring; attorney general, New Mexico Territory

SAMUEL AXTELL . . . . Governor, New Mexico Territory

LEW WALLACE . . . . Governor, New Mexico Territory

IKE ELLIS, NANCY ELLIS . . . . Shopkeepers, Lincoln; sympathetic to anti-Firm faction

JUAN PATRON
MARTIN CHAVEZ
YGINIO SALAZAR
ERASMO CHAVEZ
} Anti-Firm Hispanic residents, Lincoln County

SUSAN MCSWEEN . . . . Wife of Alexander McSween

COLONEL NATHAN DUDLEY . . . . Commander, Fort Stanton

DOCTOR BLAZER . . . . Doctor, mill owner; sympathetic to anti-Firm faction

AL COE, LOU COE . . . . Coe family members

CELLA COE . . . . Wife of George Coe

HOUSTON CHAPMAN . . . . Lawyer for McSween family

JOHN CHISUM . . . . Cattle king, New Mexico Territory

SALLIE CHISUM . . . . Niece of John Chisum

PETE MAXWELL . . . . Son of Lucien B. Maxwell, of Maxwell Land Grant

WALLY BURNS . . . . Author, *The Saga of Billy the Kid*

JUAN NEPOMUCENO GALVEZ . . . . Itinerant religious painter

George Coe. Born in Iowa, Coe was a long-time New Mexico resident, having come here with his cousins when it was still a Territory. With his cousin, Frank, he established a farm on the Ruidoso in 1877 but became caught up in the Lincoln County War in which he was part of the Tunstall-McSween faction and an associate of Billy the Kid. After the war, Coe returned to farming, became a friend of Pat Garrett's and other famous figures of the pioneering times. In his later years, he was a well-known figure in his own right, selling his fruit and his original paintings of rural churches at his roadside stand at Glen Coe. He was eighty-eight and is believed to have been the last living participant in the Lincoln County War, tales of which he loved to tell to his customers. He leaves his wife, the former Cellestina Carmichael of this city, and a daughter, Lucy Sheers of Ruidoso.

—*Roswell Daily Record*

The Kid and Me

I

You say you like this one, eh? No? This one, maybe? It's San Rafael Church at La Cueva. This here is at Guadalupe over to Fort Sumner; it's nine with the frame, seven without. But like I always tell folks, it's worth the extra two when you figure in what it's going to cost you to hunt up a frame and make certain it's the right size. When you figure in your time, the gasoline for your automobile, and what you'll pay another man for his frame, why, hellfire, you're better off paying me the nine and be done with it. I told this to a feller from Uvalde the other day, come through here with his wife on his way to Arizona—so he said—and he says, 'Well, why don't you figure in the flat tire I might get hunting up that other frame, and the patching for the tube, and maybe the tow if I happen to bend the rim and need a new one? That way,' he says, 'you're actually doing me a big favor selling me your picture and frame for nine. Maybe I should give you twelve and count myself ahead.' Then he says to me, 'Say, what hand do you do your pictures with, anyways?' So right then I knew he'd come down here on account of he'd heard about me and my finger and thumb and all. So, I just held my hand up and waggled it this way. I'm used to it, you see, after all these years. I paint with this here hand, I says, and I can still get a good grip even so. 'Is it true you took a bullet for the Kid?' says he. I answer that one of several ways, according on the situation and how I happen to be feeling that day and whether the feller might have along a pretty woman, which it happened this feller did. So I says, Well, now, if you was old Buckshot and five fellers come around a building on you, and you looked at 'em quick-like, and one of them was no more'n a boy by his looks, who would you try for, eh? Then I says, Look here, you buy the picture and this sack of apples for fifteen cents, and I'll take you up to the house and show you the finger—got it preserved in a jar. The bit of thumb wasn't worth saving.

You want to see it, too, do you? Well, come on then, and give me a ride in that smart rig of yours. Hip's giving me some trouble today, but, hellfire, I'm a good deal closer to eighty than I ever thought I'd get back when none of us figured old age into our calculations.

*

Often enough I tend to skip the preliminaries and go straight to the Kid and the war because I know goddamn well that's all folks is interested in, and some ain't even interested in the war. What they want is the Kid, the Kid, and I guess you can't blame them with all the stuff that's been put out on him the last fifty years or whatever it may be, and even that ain't really the half of it: there's still folks around here has their own Kid stories never been heard by strangers, ones passed down, some of 'em corkers, too, all about how the Kid and Jesse Evans raced their horses forty miles through broken country at night to spring a pardner from the hoosegow, and what Tom O'Folliard called Garrett after Pat shot him in the chest. The Mex people have their own stories and songs, too, more of them than any white man has heard. I used to hear some of these long ago, but now I don't go amongst them people as I once did. Stick pretty close to home, down to the stand, selling my fruit and my pictures.

Still, a good deal of this Kid stuff was picked up by a feller name of Wally Burns who come down here—oh, in the twenties, I'd say—, and he put it into a book which I understand got him considerable trouble from folks who said it wasn't true. Well, what *is* true? You really want to walk into a dance hall where some feller is up there singing a song he heard from his own pa, and it goes, 'I'll sing you a true song of Billy the Kid,' and afterwards you go up to him and say, 'Hey, there, what you sung about Billy the Kid—that ain't true.' You really want to do that? There might be better ways of getting a pool stick through your windpipe, but that'll do for me. I say there's different kinds of truth; not any old number of truths, mind you: the Kid got planted by Pat Garrett back in July of eighteen-eighty-one, and he's deader'n hell. That's the truth. But, far as the Kid's *life* is concerned, what folks thought about him then, what some of the things was he might have done, those are different things.

I know what I thought about him, and I have had many and many a thought about him down the years—way too many, it sometimes seems. But if your path crossed his, you wouldn't forget him, so when a feller like yourself asks about him you don't say, 'The Kid? What Kid?' Unless you got a reason. Also, I know the things I seen him do. There are other things I didn't see but heard about from them that was there—fellers I trust—, like Garrett who was a neighbor here for a spell, over on Eagle Creek. I spent a few days with him once when he was trying to put together an irrigation scheme, and he talked a good deal about the Kid, once I primed him with a good-sized glass of whiskey. My cousin Frank knew him well as I did, from the winter he bunked here—right over there where that low house is—and then when we was holed up a while over to San Patricio during the war. Then, way after the war was over, when the Kid was long dead and had become a hero, you might say, one night when Frank and me had got together to talk some business, why, we ended up talking about the Kid instead. Frank said what he recollected and I done the same. Before that we didn't see no point in raking up old happenings; safer to forget them. But then, all this other stuff comes along in between, including moving pictures and whatnot, and so then you get to wondering, What in hell *did* happen, anyway? But neither of us and not even the both of us put together knows the whole truth. Nobody does. Not even Garrett, who hunted the Kid down and killed him. So, if you come here for that, pardner, you come to the wrong place. Whatever the whole truth about him is, it's somewheres back there in them murdering days when he was alive.

*

I was born in Iowa, Washington County, eighteen-fifty-six. That's a fact, and it's the truth, too. Had four sisters and lots of cousins there but mostly down in Missouri just over the line, around Memphis and Queen City. Us Coes was a sprawl of a family, and for that time I believe there was quite a lot of visiting, but I don't have good recollections of them earliest years on account of the fact my mother died when I was but a tad, and after that we was split up and swapped about all over the place. Queen City was where I got to know my cousin Frank and we become fast friends, close as brothers, and stayed that way till he died three years back, April. He's buried in the family cemetery up the hill back of here. One of these old days I'll join him there.

Frank was six years older than me, but still he took a shine to me, and we did a lot of kid stuff in the fields and woods when we wasn't doing chores. It was him taught me to shoot a rifle and generally how to behave around guns, which later on come in handy. We had a deal of fun popping birds and rabbits and squirrels, and some of them ended up on the supper table. Once, Frank shot a red fox that we skinned out and tacked up on the bedroom wall, and many a night, lying next to one another, we'd look up at it in the lantern light and recollect how he gut-shot it, and it run a good ways straight across the field, but before it got to the woods it teetered over and died. One time, just helling around with a rifle, we shot a dominecker rooster and got the peedoodle whipped out of us by Frank's pa, Jasper Coe, who told us to meet him in the barn—took a harness strap to us. Frank went first and got it hardest on account of Jap figured him to have known better, but having to watch was maybe worse, since I had to get it twice, in a manner of speaking.

My own pa had some of the goddamnedest luck of any white man I ever seen—except Tunstall and McSween and that one-armed lawyer, all of 'em gunned down during the war just for being in the wrong spot. Now, you take fighting men such as Hendry Brown and Charlie Bowdre and the like, well, hellfire, you *got* to figure that one day you're going to get yours. But Tunstall and McSween, and Chapman—that was the one-armed feller—, not a one of them ever carried a sidearm nor fired a shot in the war, and all of them gunned down, senseless-like, especially old Tunstall who, when he seen a bunch of riders fanning down a draw towards him, he took off his hat and waved it at them, thinking they must be neighbors, come to pay him a visit. Oh, they paid him a visit, all right. Never knew what took him. I read a story in the papers once about a feller sitting in his rocker on his gallery somewheres, smoking his pipe, just enjoying the moment, and here come a lightning bolt out of a clear blue sky and killed him dead on the spot—pipe dropped out of his hand still smoking. How about that for bad luck, eh?

But, like I said, my pa had hell for luck: had four wives and three of them died on him, starting with my mother. The fourth lived and was mean as a rattler, and was the cause of me leaving home to come out here on account of I couldn't stand her another damn day. Pa seen it coming and had relations was driving cows down to Santa Fe and needed hands. I had no experience in that line of work, though I had been up on a horse before I was house-broke. I knew milk cows, all right, but herding head on a trail is altogether different. I didn't care what it took, though; my mind was set. Pa and me said our goodbyes where the trail forked up above Macon, him standing there holding my horse's bridle and the wind blowing so hard he had to holler up to me. 'Son,' he hollers, 'you got a good horse under you there. You got a good saddle. You got a good rifle. Best of luck to you, and goodbye.' He give old Chunk a whack on his rump and away I went, south to join up with the drive. That was just the way things was them days when so many was going west. You said your goodbyes to your kin, your neighbors and friends, and it was the same as saying, 'See you in Heaven,' or wherever else you judged they might fetch up: you never figured on seeing them again in life or hearing of them, neither, the mails then not being what they become, and most folks wasn't much hand at writing, anyways. I don't know for certain if my pa knew how. Me, I learned to write and figure well before I hit the trail, but if I've wrote ten letters since that day, I've wrote a hundred. Maybe a good half of these I wrote to Cella when I was courting her, and that took more out of me than looking at a gun pointed at me, which I have had done a time or two—just gripping that pencil like anything and licking the lead twenty times a word. You hesitate like that in a gun battle, pardner, you're a gone goose. But it must have worked for me some ways, because she married me after a fair spell, and all these years later, here we are. She's a fine woman, as you'll see when she gets back—she's up the hill visiting with her sister who is doing poorly. She don't hold with my lingo, but she knows I can't help it—just comes out that way, cuss words and all. But I go to church with her almost ever Sunday, except when I wasn't here and was off somewheres, painting my pictures of churches. So, you might say that one way or another I never truly missed a meeting.

*

After I caught up with the drive we was on the trail a good three months and ever day the same, except when something bad happened—storms, stampedes, Indians, which we never seen ourselves, though once we come upon some of their handiwork with some burnt-up wagons with just the iron parts left and some human bones scattered about and picked clean. And ever day there was dust. By Godfrey, I had never seen dust like that back in Missouri. Dust from the wind. Dust kicked up by them shit-asses we was trying to keep together. Dust from our horses and the herds of wild horses and buffalo. At the end of the day when Kip Brown—that was Jap Coe's brother-in-law—would call a halt, you'd look at the hand nearest you, and his face would be all streaky brown under his bandanna, and his eyes would be like two tiny sparks of fire. And then you knew just what you looked like.

Kip Brown had it in for me, I don't know why, since we was kin. I wasn't the best hand he had, I know that, and it took me a while before I got the general idea. But I wasn't the worst, neither: that would have been Billy Hersh, who got thrown and hit a big rock down in Kansas, and before dawn of the next day was dead. We buried him right next to the rock that killed him, figuring that if somehow his people back in Fulton was trying to find out what happened to him, we could give them something of a marker. Not likely considering everthing, but sometimes you'll do things just because they make you feel better even though they don't make much sense, which this didn't. Anyhow, as we was digging the grave and trying to straighten Billy out so he would fit in it and look a bit decent, Kip Brown was standing off to the side and kept hauling out that big clock he called a watch and mumbling about the time of day. This was just like him; he was a real shit, and, like I say, rode me like a hired burro, and not long after Billy Hersh got it things between us come to a head.

It was just an ordinary day on the trail, cows kind of quiet and lazing along, when all at once a coyote streaked out of some brush and spooked the leaders, and before I knew it I was a-fogging after that critter and snapping at him with my pistol—damn fool kid thing. But then, I think by that time all of us was a little loco from all them days under that sky that seemed to just stretch on forever and didn't have no mercy to it. Anyways, when I got back, my horse all lathered and my sidearm empty, there was Kip Brown, fat bastard, and he lit into me something terrible, called me everything from a worthless son of a bitch to a pig-fucking sodbuster, and I sat there listening to it go on and on. Finally, I got down real slow. 'What the fuck you doing off your horse,' he says. 'Get back up there and do your job before I take this here rope to you.' I had my back to him, and I reached and pulled my rifle out of the scabbard and turned around and cracked down on him. 'Listen,' I says, 'you've hazed me long enough. You're all the time worrying about the time, but by Godfrey, if you don't let up on me right quick, we're going to have to take more time yet for another funeral.' 'Course, I had no way of knowing what I looked like at that moment, but he must have seen something in my eyes that said I wasn't bluffing because he didn't say nothing, just turned his horse and nudged it into a trot, going away. Safest thing he could have done: I *would* have shot him, only I couldn't shoot him in the back, not even Kip Brown.

Well sir, that give me plenty to think about that night, wrapped up in my blanket, and other nights to come when I'd be riding night guard and out there all by my lonesome. I'd go back and back to that moment. Before it I had been wondering if I had it in me to kill a man if I had to. You naturally would wonder about it them days what with the Civil War, Quantrill, and the James gang: growing up, you heard that kind of talk all the time from older folks. What *would* you do if it come down to you or him? But now, with this business with Kip Brown under my belt, seemed like I had been given an answer, and it steadied me considerable, then and after. Meanwhile, I didn't have another ugly word out of old Kip. He cussed everbody, that being his nature, but all he ever said to me was, 'You get on over there and help Felton keep that edge,' and the like. So that part of it sunk in, too—him leaving me be. And all of this was quite shortly to come in handy when I got down to New Mexico Territory on account of down here you didn't have to look for trouble; trouble was always on your trail and a-coming hard. Here you *had* to know that if it was you or him, by Godfrey, it was going to be him if you could manage it. And even if it turned out you couldn't, at least you wouldn't die on your knees in the dirt, begging for a life that wouldn't be worth nothing to you on account of everbody would know you for a coward, and so wherever you went you wasn't safe, ever man's hand against you, as the Bible has it.

*

Things run along smooth enough down through Colorado, and we didn't have no more disasters like poor Billy or almost-disasters like me coming within a twitch of dusting Kip Brown, which most likely would have ruined life for me as well as for him. And we hadn't lost too many head time we got to Raton Pass, but everbody was Nervous Nellies about getting them up through there and down the other side. But we managed, though it was sure enough work of a different kind: we had seen mountains right along through Colorado, but it's another thing to be up in 'em along slender trails and the cows skitterish. But then, down on the other side, by Godfrey, it was like dropping down into Eden of the olden time. You come through them bluffs and there below was such a handsome spread of valleys and grassland with streams slicing through it ever which way. There's a few times in your life you remember ever after and fewer yet that you know right then you'll always carry them around with you—ever little thing clear as a bell—, and this surely was one of those.

When we had got down on the bottomland Kip Brown in his shit-ass way let us know that we was shortly to meet up with my cousin, Lou Coe. Why he kept that to himself until the very last moment, I can't say, but whatever the reason, when I saw Lou I could have cried for finding him down here from Missouri, and at the same time I felt all over again like killing Kip Brown. But I didn't, and when Lou and me had a chance to visit he told me he had a spread up on the Sugarite and his brother Al had another, and if I was tired of the trail, he would make me welcome as he knew me for a good worker. You won't have no trouble figuring out what I said to that, I'm certain, or else you ain't been listening. Anyway, Brown and the rest of the boys went on to Santa Fe with the herd, but that wasn't the last of him. Our paths was to cross yet again, and it might be a shortcut way of telling you what New Mexico Territory was like at that time if I was to say that sorry-ass feller as he was, Kip Brown was actually some deal better than many of them who kind of tumbled into this place after the Civil War.

Them days you had beat-up Confederate men coming out of Texas. You had discharged Union troops from what they called the California Column. And so right there you had a combustible condition. You had rustlers who seen all these unbranded cows wandering about, and you had many a poor man who wasn't a natural-born rustler but seen a chance to make a start by throwing what we called a long rope and slapping their brand on the ass of somebody else's cow. You had drifting cowboys, looking anywhere for work and then moving along down the trail, just restless fellers that ain't ever going to grow no moss on 'em. You had gamblers, you had whoremasters, and you had fellers wasn't any of these things but was handy with a gun—or anyways thought they was until they met up with somebody who was *really* handy and planted them in some dry wash and left them there for death to feed on, as the Psalm says. There's just something about a big, open, empty place like New Mexico that draws such folks, a goodly number of them having wore out their welcome eastward—but they was sure enough wanted back where they come from.

And then you had folks like us Coes. We wasn't angels, but we wasn't looking for trouble, neither. We wanted to be farmers is all, raise crops, run a few cows, and maybe live long enough to get to where we could tell somebody else to get out there of a bitter morning and haul a cow out of a spring mudhole. From its look, the Sugarite region was just perfect for that, and if it had turned out as peaceable as it looked, why, I believe all of us Coes would be up there yet.

As it turned out, we was already stepping on others' toes up there, only we didn't learn that till we had our first crops in that spring. Then we heard we was on land that was part of the Maxwell Land Grant—us, and the Postelwaites and Portschallers, who all come down from Missouri. So that made us squatters and not only squatters but also sodbusters trying to farm where a big-time cattleman was running his cows.

You savvy the Maxwell Land Grant? Neither do I, and after all these years I don't know anybody that does except them that has learned how to make money out of it. Them folks tend to be up there in Santa Fe—used to call 'em the Santa Fe Ring, though no longer—and they had the whole territory tied up tighter than a bull's ass: sheriffs, posses, courts, the legislature, and governor. They said, 'Git!' you got. But we didn't know none of this that first spring, only that the big-time cattleman, name of Ernest, told us to git, and while we was trying to figure out the rights of all this, he had his cowboys running cows all through our crops and gardens—just tore hell out of them. We tried everthing we could think of to keep them out. If we got wind of a drive in time, we'd quick get on our horses and ride out there, whooping and hollering, swinging blankets, firing guns in the air—trying to divert them, you see. Didn't work: we was too few, too late, and it was goddamn dangerous on account of them waddies Ernest had wasn't firing into the air; they was firing at us, and after Leon Postelwaite got winged one time, he up and quit and went back to Missouri with his family and his wife's family, and so then we was even more short-handed.

Then we tried dogging them off, which was less dangerous on account of it was dogs doing the work. Costly for the dogs, though: they got run over, gored, shot. I had two of the meanest big old dogs ever lived, Buster and Willard, who lasted longest at that game. They was so mean it was dangerous, really, to feed them. At sundown, I'd hit the triangle on the porch, and when I seen them coming I flang some big hunks of meat out in the yard and watched 'em tear into them. That way they kept up their taste for cow and connected me with providing it. They worked as a pair, just like wolves, and maybe they was part that. One time I seen 'em way out in a field, running one of Ernest's bulls, one going in at the nose, and then Buster, he shot in and tore that creature's nuts ragged, which reduced his value considerable.

But dogging didn't work finally on account of we run out of dogs, and even Buster got killed. I never did find out what happened to Willard. So then we turned to peppering the cows with birdshot—not enough to wound them, but sometimes if we could get a load into one or another of the leaders, it might be enough to turn them off, but not often, and they just kept on coming. The last straw was Postelwaite getting winged.

Then Lou and Al got together one evening and said, 'Fuck it!' They had got word from down here where Frank Coe had land, and he reported that there was good parcels suitable for crops, with good water and where there was no big-time cattleman that had everthing sewed up. There was still Indians, but they was penned up on the reservation, and there was an army fort convenient, so we would have a market for our crops. If they would throw in with him, Frank said, they could invest in a mowing machine and sell the fort all the hay they could raise. So that's

12

what we concluded to do, leaving behind all that Maxwell Land Grant mess—so we thought.

*

Fort Stanton was a four-company outfit, and we sold them our hay, corn, and fruit. My. . . . When I think back, that was a *rich* time Frank and me had, them early days on the Ruidoso. Al and Lou had families, but we was bachelors. We was working hard, sure, but business was grand up to the fort, we was young bucks, and we found reason to go up that way often as we could, load or no. There was laws against running a saloon with a whorehouse—what was called a hog ranch—within a mile of the fort. So there was a hog ranch a mile south of the fort and another just like it a mile north. Both was run by the Murphy-Dolan bunch that come into the territory with the California Column. They was backed from the start by Tom Catron and the Santa Fe Ring, though we didn't find this out until later. What we did know was that the Murphy-Dolan bunch was the big supplier of goods for the ranchers and farmers for many miles around. They was called the Firm, and when you went there for your supplies, they had you by the short-hairs, pardner. But, as I say, we was young, and was having such a hell of a time up to the fort we didn't give much thought to the Firm or who they answered to up in Santa Fe, where we had never been. Shows you how much you're willing to overlook when your blood's hot, and them days ours was smoking.

Them hog ranches tended to be pretty rough places, but, considering, they was well enough run. You could get drunked-up, all right, but there was no busting up the furniture or shooting out the lights. You could dance with the gals and go upstairs with them—a buck for a quickie, five to shoot the moon—, but there was no bashing them. You wanted to mix it up, Jimmy Dolan didn't give a shit if you killed each other, long as it happened outside: knives, bullwhips, guns, log chains. Dolan managed both places for the Firm—tough, wire-haired little son of a bitch. He'd take on anybody, many of them half again his size, but then, he carried lead rolls in his hands and had his boys there to back him. Once you seen what they could do to a man who got out of line, you didn't want any of that game: they would bust you up so bad you was worthless for months.

If you was a soldier, when your friends got you back to the fort, you'd be thrown in the guardhouse, but at least there you was out of the rain and would get your bread and water. But if you was a hand, who was there to take you in? Frank had a feller name of Tim Terwilliger got into it with a soldier and just wouldn't let go of it. Then he carried on with one of Jimmy Dolan's boys, and they broke his back. Frank had to turn him out, said he wasn't running no hospital, and I couldn't have him lying around my bunkhouse, neither—didn't have the room or an extra hand to see to him. Somehow—I don't know how—Tim survived, and we later heard he was running a whorehouse in Tascosa, where he must have had plenty of competition, that being a tough little town.

After a night at the hog ranch the soldiers had barracks to go to. Rest of us had to mount up and ride for home, wherever home was. If Frank and me wasn't up there with the team and wagon and judged we wasn't in no condition to ride home, why, we'd just go down into the woods on the Bonito, put the hobbles on the horses and crawl into our blankets to sleep the worst of it off. With the team it was only a bit more complicated and we managed. But one night in green-up time it snowed like hell and we just crawled in together and hugged each other hard till daylight come. Blood or no, you can get to know a feller pretty good that way.

Me, I got good and stuck on a gal up there name of Rosalita. Once that happened, when I'd be back at my place it was hard to keep my mind on my work: instead, I'd be scheming to get back up to the fort and give it to her. She was younger than me—couldn't have been sixteen, if that—and eager. So, when I could get away from work, I'd run my horse up there about as fast as I thought he could take it, wait my turn when I had to, and then dance with Rosalita. But she knew what I was there for, and we didn't take that many turns around the floor before we went up the stairs—

> Say, Buffalo gals, can't you come out tonight,
> Come out tonight, O, come out tonight.
> Say, Buffalo gals, can't you come out tonight,
> And dance by the light of the moon—

That was a popular song they had back then, and whenever I chance to hear it now, it puts me in mind of Rosalita and them rich days long ago.

Sometimes, when she'd get through with me I couldn't hardly swing my leg up into the saddle. But you know, that's a real good feeling, though it's a young man's good feeling: you'd put your boot in the stirrup, but when you went to put your weight on it, it would go kind of jelly-like. But you'd keep on, swinging your other leg up and over, and maybe Frank would be there, laughing the while, but finally you'd make it and be sitting there with a good horse under you and your legs quivery and your pecker sore. But you was thinking, *Damn!* that was a hell of a ride Rosalita give me, and, by Godfrey, if you ain't already begun thinking about getting back up there for another shot at sweetie. Rosalita give me my first dose, but I didn't really mind: wasn't no worse than a bad cold and a lot more pleasure.

*

Such things don't go on forever, do they? But back then I didn't see no reason why not. But one day in spring, close to sundown,

I seen a rider come down off the San Patricio road, and I watched while he come across the river. I was finishing chores and waited till I could recognize him to be Winn Rigney, who was book-keeper for the Firm. I'd seen him around, mostly in the store over to Lincoln. He raised his hand slow and asked if he might stay the night as it was coming on dark, and he was yet a ways from town. I said, sure enough, if he didn't mind cold pork and day-old beans and a blanket on the floor, as the bunkhouse was full. Said he didn't, and that was that.

Rigney always struck me as a quiet feller, especially next to Murphy, who was drunked-up most of the time and didn't make sense and Jimmy Dolan with his lead rolls and looking for trouble, and while we ate he hardly said a word. But when I got the jug down and turned up the lamp, then it was me hardly said anything—didn't have a chance on account of that drink primed Winn's pump good, and for a spell all I did was sit back and listen to his lamentations, as in the Bible.

This here, he told me, motioning back towards the fort, was his last piece of work for the Firm. Said he was quitting and in the morning was going directly from here back to his people in Texas. Murphy had sent him over to the fort to talk the com-mander out of barring the Firm from ever doing business again on government property on account of Dolan and his boys having just crippled a brevet-major over some trifle. 'This here's the last straw for me,' he says. 'I been covering up how bad the business has been let go, but now with this, Tom Catron and them up to Santa Fe will quick find out what's what, and that will be the end of Murphy.' Dolan, too, he said, who wasn't nothing but a barroom bully with no head at all for business. Things had gotten to a state where even McSween, who was their lawyer, had already quit and was talking to the Englishman, Tunstall, about going partners. When he finally quit talking, I give him another good cupful and asked how come him to stop by here and unload all this. 'You was on my way out of here,' he said, 'and was a lantern in the dark. I didn't figure you to murder me in my bed.'

Next morning when I come down out of the field, I seen him saddling up. Coffee? I says, but he says no, so I go down to the gate to let him through. 'Coe,' he says, 'if McSween and Tunstall mean to go up against Murphy, there will be the devil to pay: Tom Catron and his bunch ain't going to let their man go to the wall. You and your kin had best be mighty careful.' So that's how we learned about the beginnings of what come to be called the Lincoln County War.

II

Some while after this Frank went over to Lincoln for supplies, and when he went into the Firm's store he seen some new faces there and more of them still across the way at the Wortley Hotel: hard faces, they was, belonging to heavy-armed men that seemingly didn't have nothing to do but look ugly at you when you went past. In amongst them Frank seen my old boss, Kip Brown, and signed to him, but all Kip did was turn his head and spit.

That was the commencement of a strange summer, where nothing much seemed to happen, but underneath a lot was boiling up. Weather was likewise: there was a lot of stock-still days, not much wind, lots of clouds with heavy mutterings—very unusual for this country. But it was looking like it might be a fair year for crops, and we was itching to put our mowing machine into operation and begin hauling hay to the fort. The hog ranches was still buttoned up on account of the beating of the brevet-major, so that made it feel even deader and stiller down here. I must say I missed my times with Rosalita and wondered what become of her. Once in a while me and Frank would go over to San Patricio, where they had two little cantinas, but it was different. The new padre there had done a good job scaring hell out of the gals, and you was a lucky feller if you could catch a kiss outside in the dark when they'd hold a *baile*—that's an old-time dance with fiddles and guitars, quite a bit of fun, really. But we was used to a more lively time, I guess, and all this felt kind of tame. Later on, I come to be goddamn glad about quiet little San Patricio, but not that summer. One thing, though: that was where me and Frank begun to learn the fiddle. Fact.

We had a feller working for us name of Erasmo Chavez who was from San Patricio, and you know how it is: you see a man doing only one thing—shoeing horses, say—, and you don't ever think of him doing nothing else, like he just went to bed with his hammer in hand and his mouth full of nails and got up in the mornings the same. But when we commenced going over to San Patricio, why, there was Erasmo, playing fiddle at the *bailes*, and, my, how he could play! Quite a surprise for us, and it raised him considerable in our estimation. So we got to thinking—Frank first—, well, if a Mex blacksmith can do that, it can't be that hard, and maybe if we could learn it from him, we might become more welcome over there. Didn't quite turn out that way on account of the fiddle is kind of onrey-like: you get cross-wise with it, and it'll sound like a coyote caught in a trap. You got to *go* some if you want to play it. Well, we started on it, anyway, and when we'd go over there Erasmo would show us a little something. Frank had a beat-up fiddle belonged to his pa, and between one thing and another we begun to make friends with it. But that's another story, a peacetime story, and peacetime was a mighty long ways off in coming to Lincoln County.

*

Tunstall, his was the first killing in the war, shot right out of his saddle, like I said. He was an odd duck out here, him and McSween, who become his business partner that summer. Tunstall was more different than McSween, who was at least American, but Tunstall come over from England; supposed to be from some big family there. He dressed all in wool clothes no matter what the weather and wore these funny little shoes that looked like they wanted to be a boot but come up short. I never really learned to savvy his lingo, except for a word here and there, but then, he didn't last long enough for us to get well acquainted. Him and McSween was sure-enough go-getters who sized up the conditions here and seen it was a place they could make money. In that way they was no different from them other newcomers I mentioned—no different than us Coes, come to think of it—, except they thought big where we never did. When McSween quit the Firm and was looking around for somebody who thought like him, there was Tunstall looking for the same thing. Also, McSween knew John Chisum, another think-bigger who had just got his ass peppered pretty good by a bunch of smaller ranchers over in the Seven Rivers region who didn't take kindly to his big ideas, and he was looking to expand his operations over this way. So when these three fellers found each other and calculated to throw in together and go up against the Firm—well, there you had all the makings you could want for a hellfire dustup which just kept on building and building all through that dead-quiet summer.

And when I say "building" I mean just that, because Tunstall and his new partners didn't waste a minute but went right to work slapping together a big new store at the east end of town and stocking it with the same goods as the Firm at the other end of the street, only they was offering these at lower prices. When the Firm seen that, what they did was to put a pool hall and saloon in their store, hoping to keep their trade that way. So then, you had hammering at both ends of town and more and more of them hard-looking cases drifting in. Only now some of them was also to be found down at the new store, and still others was known to be out at Tunstall's ranch.

One day Frank come back from Lincoln and stopped by my place and said we needed to sit down and try to figure out what we was going to do, on account of there was big trouble coming, and we had already taken sides by talking with Tunstall about switching our custom to him. 'Tunstall and me was standing on the portal of his store,' he said, 'talking through this, and there was a feller there painting one of the big wooden shutters they got. We had to move so he could get at its backside with his brush, and when he swung that thing out, I seen something.' He tapped me on the chest and said, 'Son, in between them wood slabs, front and back, there's a sheet that ain't wood—it's all *metal*. There is going to be a war.'

I was maybe more of a hothead than him—younger man and all—, and I said that if it had to come to that, I'd just as soon take Tunstall's side on account of I had rather shoot Kip Brown in the belly than the back. It was kind of a dumb thing to say, as I had no real idea of what 'war' meant, nor what it would mean to us Coes. But then, looking back, I don't know as anybody *really* knew what a war would mean. Except maybe the Kid.

*

On towards the end of the year, which was staying on mild and still—might have been November—Frank and me was on the way to Lincoln with the team and wagon for supplies, the first we was to purchase from Tunstall, McSween, and Chisum, the new firm. And here come Tunstall himself and another rider, clattering along the road behind us, and Tunstall keeps coming at a real good clip while the other man drops back. Then Tunstall sees who it is and reins in alongside. "Howdy," he says or something like, and Frank tells him we was on our way to his store. Tunstall smiles real big and says how we won't never be sorry we give him our custom, that he trades fair—fair prices for first-rate goods. 'Value received for value paid,' he says. Then the other rider comes on a bit, but still he don't come up level. We keep looking over our shoulders like you would anyways, but we was especially edgeful them days, and so Tunstall motions him to come along, and he does some, but I can see he still has a rein on a dancy little sorrel filly. So Tunstall coaxes him further, trying to be sociable, and he does come up further yet, but still he keeps a distance.

Then we got a good look at him, and was both of us surprised: he was but a boy, and that was what stuck in our minds ever after. He was sitting that sorrel real nice, no daylight at all between his seat and the leather, which is what you see in a good horseman at a trot. Had on a heavy sweater and was armed with a carbine, pistol, and two cartridge belts, and had a Mex sugarloaf hat considerable beat up: nothing unusual here, including the arms, things being what they was at that time. But it was the face that stopped you, or rather the eyes in the face: peach fuzz around the mouth and chin, rabbit-like front teeth, which you could see on account of his mouth being open a bit with the jouncing of the sorrel. But when he looked at you, you didn't see none of them things no more because of the eyes. Real light gray they was, but didn't seem somehow to go with the face. They wasn't young, and they wasn't old, neither. They didn't seem to have no age to them whatever. It was like when they first opened they already knew everthing about the world they was ever going to need, about life and about death, and about what all it was going to take—the kind of knowing that comes to you and me along the trail where you pick up something here and another thing further along, and so on; like I done, for instance, when I looked at old Kip Brown and knew for certain I could kill him. Learning is a slow thing, seems like, and takes living along down the years. Not with him, though. His eyes said he was just *born* with all that knowing.

I may as well cut in here to say that I shot a man in the war. He lived, but he didn't live on. Some while after, he died, just of what I don't know, and I never tried to find out, on account of I wanted to believe it wasn't me that took him off but something else I had nothing to do with: that ain't the sort of thing you want to pack along with you down the years—leastways, I don't. With the Kid, though, if it mattered at all, it mattered like losing at monte, which he did from time to time, like all gamblers. Several times I chanced upon him, coming out of a cantina where he'd been playing, and you couldn't tell from his eyes how it had gone for him in there. It had just *gone*, is all. That was his way with everthing, far as I could tell, including death. His eyes looked like they knew all about it, what it was like for the other man, and what it would be like for himself, too, which, considering how he lived, might be the next minute: no fear, no regrets, no *nothing*. Just the pure knowing, which don't take sides. Often, even yet, I'll think back on him for no special reason. Might be down at the stand, selling my pictures and my fruit—like I done with you—and instead of keeping my mind on my business, I'll be thinking of him, dying on the floor in Pete Maxwell's bedroom over there to Fort Sumner. And then I'll go on and picture him dead and them eyes still open,—and they *was* open, too: I have Garrett's word on that, for he told me they had to weight them down with coins when they laid him out—open on all he already knew about that condition. Kind of spooky when you think of it that way, ain't it?

Old man Charlie Foor, who used to take folks around that graveyard where they planted the Kid, he would say that what spooked him was them front teeth that made him look like he was laughing when he wasn't. 'Think of him down there in the clay,' old Charlie would say, laying it on some, 'still laughing away after all these years.' I believe Charlie picked up a fair bit of change with that routine he worked out. He did it for that writer, Burns, who put it in the book. Me, though, it was the eyes that stayed. And this time I'm telling you of, when me and Frank first got a look at him, was a remarkable moment because of that.

Anyway, when he'd come level with us there on the road Tunstall says to him, 'These are some fine customers of ours, on their way to the store for supplies.' Then he turns back to us and says, 'Gentlemen, this here is a new hand, just in from Arizona. He goes by Kid Antrim, but we call him Billy.'

*

We called him 'Billy,' and we called him 'Kid,' but I never heard 'Billy the Kid,' until after most of the shooting had quit and Lew Wallace put out a wanted poster that said, 'Billy the Kid.' I never knew where 'Antrim' come from, never give it any thought. Them days out here lots of folks was traveling under names different from what they'd been born under. Later on, the Kid told Wallace he was Billy Bonney, and he signed some letters that way, though I never seen these myself. Where he picked that name up is a mystery—or is to them wants to chase after such things. And there was another name yet he was known by, 'El Chivato,' which is Kid in Mexican.

One thing we found out quick was that he could speak Mexican like he was one. Him and Erasmo Chavez hit it right off that way when Chavez, him, and me and Frank McNabb was all together in the bunkhouse that first winter, and half the time we didn't know what the Kid and Erasmo was talking about, unless the Kid told us, which he did from time to time. He was just naturally at home around them folks, talked their lingo, sang their songs, danced with their gals, loved their chow, which many a white man didn't, me for one. And he had more señoritas on his string than you could count—and maybe he didn't know the number himself—, beginning that winter when he commenced going over to San Patricio where Erasmo introduced him around. When Garrett and his possemen was chasing him all over the territory after the big shootout we said the Kid was probably having a far rougher time dodging jealous girlfriends than lawmen. Somebody asked him once was that so, and he just sort of laughed, careful-like. Way afterwards, when he was long dead and all kinds of talk had commenced, it begun to get around that one of his girlfriends had been Sallie Chisum, who was John Chisum's niece. Now, it ain't my job to defend the Kid against anything. Telling what I know is one thing, and defending him another, but in this here matter I got to step in and say no such a thing ever happened.

A reputation, I figure, is like a magnet—draws all kinds of iron filings, and here it's like with the Kid's reputation as a killer: if he killed eight men or whatever, then he killed twenty-one. If he put the spurs to thirty Mex gals, he put 'em to Sallie Chisum, sure. And why? Because he was the Kid, and the Kid wasn't only a killer, he was a lady-killer. Well, listen here, pardner, I knew Sallie Chisum, and she was never that sort. She was a *peach*, just beautiful: blonde hair and rosy cheeks, and you could tell she was well set up underneath all them clothes women used to wear them days, even when riding.

When I met her I was riding regular with the Kid, and she must have been eighteen or so. Chisum was a bachelor and needed a white woman to run that big operation he had at South Spring, outside Roswell, and young as she was, Sallie fit the bill perfect. Chisum was a sure-enough cattle king, and lived like it: big old sprawl of a house with a long double row of cotton-woods leading to it, two galleries, front and back, and a dining room that ever night was set for twenty-five, even if nobody in particular was expected. And Sallie run that whole shebang like she had put it together herself. Several times I dropped in there with the Kid and some of our bunch, and when we would catch a look at Miss Sallie, why, we'd go straight out to the well and the bunkhouse and do the best we could, slicking our hair back with water, smacking the dust out of our clothes, trying to look spruce, you see. The Kid was no different in that way. But you didn't have to be no mind reader to see him and Miss Sallie found each other interesting. They was both kids, and he was this hard-riding boy who was said to be a killer with a price on his head. I ain't an expert on how women think—Cella will back me on that—, but if you can picture Sallie Chisum managing her uncle's place and living in a world just full of men that was all rough, dusty customers who might not have been in a creek for a bath in some while—all of us smelling of horse sweat and dust and whiskey and whatnot. And then all of a sudden, here's the Kid. He's small, he's her age, he has got manners, and somehow he's gotten himself presentable. And while many of us was sneaking looks at Sallie like we'd love nothing better in this old world than to just tear her bloomers off and give it to her under the dining room table, the Kid was never like that, never grinned ugly at her or the like. So, he would have been quite a welcome change, wouldn't you think? I would, and I seen the way they would look at each other when he come in the room for supper.

It's true they spent time together. We all seen that. When the Mex help cleared off the dishes and the boys was having their coffee, then maybe Chisum might take a glass with them, but maybe not, as he was ever careful that way. Then he would excuse himself, and you wouldn't see him again that night, nor the next morning. Rest of us would push our chairs back and head for the bunkhouse or out to our bedrolls if we had to, and the Kid and Sallie would sit around and talk. If the weather was good, they'd go out on the front gallery for the night breeze. I don't know what they done out there in the quiet by themselves. No man does. I do know what they *didn't* do. Out back, the rest of us would think about what they might be doing, used to talk about it, and you know yourself how talk will run to dirt when it's just a bunch of men without no women, gabbing away. One time, though, when there was a good wind blowing our way, we heard her call him Billy, and shortly after, he sung a song I heard him sing before, a Mexican one called 'Consuelo.' Real nice tune and his voice high and clear in the dark.

So, there's the true story of the Kid and Sallie Chisum, whatever of that old talk you might have heard. As for the rest of his gals, it might have been different, though he was ever polite. Fine dancer, sang some when minded, but there's no doubt he was a randy rooster and remained so till the night he went down.

*

Like I said a bit ago, he bunked right over there that first winter, him, me, Erasmo Chavez, and Frank McNabb. But he wasn't working for us; was working for Tunstall. Tunstall had taken on so many hands he'd run out of bunks and asked us if we could put the Kid up, said he'd take the charges off our store bill. We happened to have an extra bunk, so we said, sure. Besides, the Kid was good company when he was around—neat and tidy. A bunkhouse of fellers can get nasty if you ain't got regulations on who does what and when, and we wasn't always that particular about chores like washing up after supper and the like. His setup was different, though, bunk covers pulled up and his possessions stowed underneath. If the rest of us could have been shamed, I guess we would have been by the way he kept himself, but mostly we just went on as we was until a day come when things had got so bad we'd throw open the door and get out the bucket and broom.

Most days he was up a bit before the rest of us and riding over the hills to Tunstall's. When he come back at sundown, he looked pretty much as he had when riding out, so it didn't seem like he was doing much ranch work, if he was doing any, and that he was on Tunstall's payroll because he could handle a gun. And here it's like with him and women—just a lot of horseshit talk, most of it from experts who couldn't hit a cow in the ass with a barn board: the Kid could do this, the Kid could do that, the Kid was the fastest ever, the Kid was a sure-shot.

Well, he was good, damn good. Of the men I seen shoot, Hendry Brown was maybe better, Fred Waite was good, and

Annie Oakley best of all. It's a question of what you're talking about, shooting at someone who's shooting back, or at a target. As for sure-shots, I never seen one and don't believe such exist: nobody hits a hundred percent nor even ninety, whether it's at a man, a bear, or a bottle. There was a Mex feller up near White Oaks years back, claimed he seen the Kid throw a tin can in the air, twirl his pistol on his trigger finger, then hit it six times 'fore it hit the ground. Can't be done, unless the Kid flang it a hundred feet up, and even there he'd have to recover and set himself and aim. Wally Burns wrote that Frank told him the Kid would ride along at his place, shooting birds off fence posts and hitting four of six. Well, that night I mentioned before—when me and Frank got to swapping recollections of the Kid—, I said did he tell Burns that yarn, and Frank said he never. But then, later that night when we'd been at the jug a bit, he commenced to laughing and said maybe he had after all. So there you are again: what in hellfire *is* the truth here, anyhow? Was it Frank telling Burns a yarn? Was it Burns himself making up a good story? Was it old Frank with some whiskey in him, thinking back and wondering what he did tell Burns? Or is it me now, disremembering what was said that night, because I hadn't been drinking river water, neither. By Godfrey, life is a tanglement, ain't it?

*

One thing's sure, though: the Kid, good as he was, was no sure-shot and never done many of the things they said, including them twenty-one killings. Just to give you one example that comes to mind is his killing of Texas Red Grant over to Fort Sumner. Oh, he killed Grant, all right, no doubting that one. But the story had him putting six shots in Grant's forehead in a pattern could covered by a silver dollar. Sure, he was shooting point-blank and was firing that .41 Thunderer he carried—good gun for him on account of it was kind of compact and light, and he had hands small as a boy. Still, it's a .41 and would have some action to it. And then you got to figure old Grant wasn't just standing still there but would be falling after the first hit, and so the Kid would be trying to foller his man with his pistol. Six shots inside the circle of a silver dollar? Good story, but no sale here. True enough, remarkable things will happen in a gun battle. Take Buckshot Roberts, who was known to be fearless but not an especially magnificent shot. That was *some* shooting he done at Blazer's Mill: crippled or killed quite a bunch of men. But he missed a lot, too. So did the Kid, and they was firing at each other not ten paces apart. What are the chances for all that happening, do you calculate—or ever happening just that way again?

The thing that set the Kid off here was this: whatever the conditions, he was always the same—steady. Least that was my experience being around him in some pretty tight conditions, and them days, once the sides had formed up, seemed like ever day brung a tight condition. But the Kid went through them all the same, never nervy. Frank said the same. Everybody went around heavy-armed, and killing was in the air so you could *smell* it. Not just burned powder but blood, in a manner of speaking. First thing you done in the morning was strap on that cartridge belt and look to your sidearm and rifle, meanwhile thinking, Is this my last sunup? So, you was jumpy all the time. When you was out on the trail hunting the enemy, if somebody was to knock a coffeepot into the fire, everbody jumped, horses, too, and men would go for their guns, and so forth. And these, mind, ain't schoolboys I'm mentioning here. These are hard men, *hard* men: Charlie Bowdre, Doc Scurlock, Hendry Brown, Fred Waite—we called him Dash—, part Choctaw, part white man, and tough as a Mexican saddle all through. And I seen Fred flinch a time or two in a desperate spot, but never the Kid. He was as cool as a creek going on cold. When the coffeepot clattered into the fire, he might look over to see what it was and maybe have him a chuckle, smoking his cigarette. Eyes never seemed to change. You know how if we was sitting here as we now are, and I was to flang my hand up like so—sudden. Well, now, I seen you startle a bit there and your eyes get big quick, then flare down. Well, I don't recollect seeing that in him. Don't seem natural somehow, but anyway, that's what set him off from the rest: when the shooting commenced, he stayed collected. He might miss his aim, but he'd keep his eyes on his man and didn't appear to have the concerns the rest of us did. That don't mean he was a fool that took chances and let himself get shot at in the open: if there was cover, he took it, same as any man. What I mean is, if there wasn't any available, he would keep working his weapon till he could make a break for it. When you think back, that ain't the worst choice you could come to: if you break and run, you only got that one hope: that you don't get hit before you get to the boulder or whatever it may be; where, if you was to keep a-snapping, you might hit your man, or you might cause *him* to be the one to give ground.

I can't tell you what went into his steadiness. Closest I can come is what Frank said once. Said the Kid told him that when he was yet a tad and hanging around some tough older hombres over to Silver City, he found out that a good way to get bully-ragged all the time was to run off. I don't know that this explains too much, except maybe he had to take some lickings before he come to believe that if he was to begin showing up with a pistol in his waistband, a bigger feller might want to think again before slapping little Billy around. Course he'd have to be able to work that thing—and how he learned that is what we don't know.

*

Them days these hills hereabouts had more cover than they do now with all the ranches and farms and this terrible drought we got, and we done a good deal of hunting in the valley that winter, the Kid and me. When he wasn't over to Tunstall's or tomming around over to San Patricio, we went after deer, bear, and turkeys. I may say I wasn't ashamed of my own bag at day's end, and once I got three deer and a turkey in an afternoon. We'd dress what we got, lay them up in the barn, and let 'em freeze. Then we'd haul them to the fort and sell them to Dudley, who was the commander. Still no hog ranches there, and I would think back on Rosalita, but I never said a word on this or nothing like it to the Kid. He just wasn't the sort that talked women. Friendly enough, like I said, but there was a something about him that wasn't inviting in private ways. Once I asked him where he come from, and he kind of laughed a little and said, 'Oh, lots of places,' and that had to do you. You didn't want to poke around into his business, same as you wouldn't want to jam a stick down a rattler's hole to find out how many buttons he's got.

III

They ought to have called it the "Possemen's War" on account of that's how it was fought out—between rivaling gangs of possemen that was gathered to serve warrants on men of the other side. It all depended on who owned the sheriff, if it was the Firm or Tunstall, McSween, and John Chisum. If the sheriff was Brady or Dad Peppin, they got paid by the Santa Fe Ring, and their possemen was given quick titles like Special Deputy or Acting Deputy or Special Assistant to the Acting Deputy, and when the sheriff signed the warrant and give out all the titles and badges, off they'd go—sometimes thirty of them—to serve that warrant on an enemy man. The warrants was lawful—except they really wasn't as there wasn't no law in the county—, but ever one knew the idea was to put the other side out of business, permanent. So, what you had was these gangs of heavy-armed men, helling around, trying to serve these shit-ass pieces of paper but really just looking to murder their enemies and then claim the 'wanted' men had tried to escape the law. And the longer this went on, the more foolish them warrants become, until on towards the end of it nobody bothered no more with warrants and badges: you just hunted your enemies, and when you found 'em you started in a-snapping at each other.

I believe there was many of us on both sides was real surprised by the whole goddamn thing: by how quick it roared up, by all the murderings and executions, and then by the way it all come together in the big shootout in Lincoln that come near to blotting out the town, and turning the county into a wilderness with all the settlers and their families run off. I know for a fact I was that surprised, surprised too that I got caught up in this hellacious mess when all I wanted to do was run my farm and get up to the hog ranch. Frank was the same.

I recollect a particular time when it come over me that I didn't have no idea of what I was doing ever day nor sometimes even any idea of where I was. Us Regulators—that's what our posse called themselves—was down close to Old Mexico, below the Seven Rivers area, hitting the high places on the trail of some of the Firm's men we had been told was somewheres around there. We'd been at this two, three days, getting madder by the mile, horses getting blowed, your ass getting pounded, and ever time we judged we had their trail sure, then it went cold. Night was coming on, and we stopped at some tiny Mex village—just a couple of jacals thrown together there—, figuring we needed feed and water for our horses. We was sitting around the fire, maybe eight of us, worrying down some mutton that was ripe and drinking the mescal bought from the Mex sheepmen—dirty, mad, and lost. Then Dash Waite looks across at Middleton and says, 'Jack, where in hell are we now, do you figure?' And Middleton, who was supposed to know that territory, just threwed up his hands and didn't say nothing. There wasn't nothing to say. Wasn't nothing to do, neither, but try to put the condition out of mind with the mescal, which did help some in the short run. But we was sure enough a sorry bunch of buggers next morning when we turned back west and give up on our enemies. That mescal can be some ugly shit, even without the worm.

*

Well, Tunstall's killing begun it all, as everbody around here will agree; happened at the end of the first winter when the Kid was working for him. Tunstall got wind that Sheriff Brady was to swear out a warrant on him on account of he was now partners with McSween, who was said to have stolen from the Firm when he was its lawyer. So, before a posse could get out to his place and arrest him and round up his stock, he decides he's going to ride into Lincoln and talk with Brady to see what all this amounted to. Like I said, he didn't carry no arms, but he knew things had come to a pass where only a fool would go anywheres in the county without some kind of protection, which on this day was the Kid, Dick Brewer, Jack Middleton, Dash Waite, and a man named Widenham or Widenam. They hardly cleared the ranch when they flushed a fine flock of turkeys and must have seen them as dinner, because Dick Brewer give a whoop, and off they all went, leaving their boss by himself. And sure enough, in that condition, soon as the boys disappeared over the ridge, here comes a big posse, just burning down a draw towards him, whooping themselves, and popping off a few celebrating shots. Up in the hills Dick and the Kid heard the commotion and turned back, but they was too late. Soon as they come back to the ridgetop they seen the posse and Tunstall, who had reined in by a clump of junipers and had lifted his hat, same as to say, 'Howdy, neighbors.' Then Buck Morton stands up in his saddle and shoots Tunstall in the chest, and he done a kind of somersault into them junipers but bounced back out again, and went face down in the dirt. I had all this from the Kid later on when we was spending some time hiding out in San Patricio, and he said he knew straight off his boss was dead as hell, and he grabbed the bridle of Dick's horse and said wasn't no use charging down there to get themselves killed. So, they just had to sit there behind some trees and watch what went on.

Well, they boiled up around the body, and Tom Hill jumped down and blew out the back of Tunstall's head and then spun around and killed Tunstall's horse, a nice bay the Kid had given him not long before. The Kid said it screamed like anything and fell over. Then they drug Tunstall over to the bay, took the saddle from it and put it under what was left of Tunstall's head, like it was a pillow, and fetched his hat and put it on the bay, so it looked like a man and his horse had got tired and decided to lay down together and take a nap. And while they was up to all this they was laughing like devils and firing into the air. I've forgotten now the names of them that was there besides Morton, Tom Hill, Frank Baker, Jesse Evans, Buckshot Roberts—couldn't forget him—, and George Hindman. Anyways, when it was all over and they had rode off, the Kid, real quiet, says to Dick Brewer, 'Dick, I'm going to get ever last one of them and the man who sent them.' Well, he didn't quite. But he got some, all right.

*

This happened pretty close to where we're sitting just now, back above the family cemetery. Somebody, way back then, put a pile of stones on the spot, and far as I know it's there yet. If my hip would allow, I could take you to it, but no matter: the thing was done and done terrible and put a brand on the war nothing could change—in fact, it's there yet: old families here can't ever seem to forget who was on which side and what was done by this man or that. But when you think back, you have to wonder why it begun that way? I mean, it's one thing to kill a man and then let it out that you had to 'cause he was trying to escape the law. And in a warlike way you could even say that killing Tunstall made sense, on account of the fact that his was the money behind the new operation: McSween didn't have near that kind of money, and Chisum's money was all in cows. Kill Tunstall and you like to close up that upstart outfit quick. But the *way* they done it? Blow out a man's brains after he's dead, shoot his horse, and rig 'em up like they done? Maybe they was drunked-up, I don't know. But whatever devilment went into it, it stayed in there all the way through to the last killing, which was that one-armed lawyer I mentioned, Chapman. Mighty few prisoners was taken that lived to tell of it, and there wasn't no rules at all on how to fight. I believe there was *some* rules at least in that World War they had some years back. I heard a feller in Lincoln that had been in it say us and the Germans got together nights, after the day's shooting was done, and talked and give one another cigarettes and chocolates and the like. Not here in Lincoln County. And this business they got now in the moving pictures, where two men face off and draw their guns? Well, I don't know that *ever* happened out here, but it sure as hell never happened in our war. There was shootouts, sure, where men was facing each other, and there was the big shootout. But there was a lot more murders and executions, which is what I would name what happened to Tunstall.

Word of his killing got back to Lincoln pretty quick, but it was some days before they got up here to collect the body. Me and Frank knew it was somewhere around, but concluded not to go anywhere near it on account of getting involved in that way. I may say I wasn't in any rush to make no such discoveries. Finally I did see the body, as it was brought down past my place; had it strapped over a mule on account of they couldn't get a wagon up there, and it was a horrible sight without no back to the head and having got clawed up considerable by animals, and then brought down through heavy brush. Frank and me give them our wagon and went the rest of the way into town with them, and folks there was naturally shocked at the way it looked.

Well, they done the best they could with him and wadded some rags in the back of his head, which had looked shrunk, and me and Frank and the Kid carried the box out behind his store to where they buried him. Nobody from the upper end of town come to the burial, including Sheriff Brady, which in reason he should have, if just to bear witness that the warrant had been served and justice done. But he never, and for all I know he was gathered

37

with Jimmy Dolan and the rest of the outfit, having a celebration over the fact that they had done wiped out the enemy's chief.

McSween and his wife was there at graveside, and he was considerable shaky, while she was fired up, telling everbody who would listen that she had told Tunstall and her husband not to try to go up against the Firm, that no good could come of it. I don't recollect the Kid saying a word nor even looking specially gloomy, as many was. Nor did he say anything later on when our side—which maybe until that moment didn't even recognize it was a side—got together at Uncle Ike Ellis's store at the lower edge of town. There was plenty of high talk there, all about how we had to saddle up now and get after them murdering fuckers and kill them all. But McSween tried to make them quit that sort of thing: he was a lawyer and a Bible-minded man, and said the guilty men should be caught and brought to trial. Nobody else was of that sort of mind, and when he seen that, he said he wouldn't stand for no more such talk in his presence, and left the place and went home to Mrs. McSween—which couldn't have been no picnic, neither, given her opinions.

That was when we formed the Regulators and picked Dick Brewer as our chief. He was a strapping, handsome feller, and well liked. Also, he held grudges against the Firm on account of when he had worked for them they had treated him shitty and he knew they charged high, just because they could. He was one of the first to switch over to the new firm and like the Kid thought high of Tunstall. When they went out to fetch the body, he was with them, but unlike the Kid, he was riled and itching to get on the trail of the killers, which is shortly what they concluded to do. Dick led them eastward, following a rumor that had the possemen heading toward the Pecos Valley and on that way out of the county so they could hide out till things simmered down.

I never did hear where they run across the possemen's trail— somewheres out that way—, but when they sighted them there commenced a running battle with starts and stops that went on quite a ways. Then somehow Buck Morton and Frank Baker got split off from their pals, and the Regulators went after them two and shot Baker's horse from under him, and they give up. This was below Chisum's ranch, and Dick took their prisoners over there where they watered and fed the horses, and Dick borrowed a horse for Baker to ride back to Lincoln. Both Chisum and Sallie was gone somewheres, but I don't believe it would have made a difference if they'd been there: the Regulators and especially Dick was in an ugly mood; you got to remember they had just been to Tunstall's burial. Baker and Morton was both scared as hell, but there was nobody to help them except a feller riding with the Regulators, name of McCluskie, who was sort of friends with Baker, and Baker begged him to protect him for old time's sake. McCluskie said he would, if he could. He wasn't a young feller, and I don't rightly know how he come to be riding with that bunch, but I believe he may have been working at Tunstall's store. Anyways, they left South Spring and hit north and west into Blackwater Canyon. It gets pretty narrer back in there, and so they was considerable spread out where the canyon jags left around a rock slide and a clump of cottonwoods. Dick was back towards the end of the file and Hendry Brown and the Kid was frontwards, just behind the prisoners and old McCluskie.

Everbody situated to know what happened next is long dead, and what they saw gone into the dark with them. And maybe even at the time it might have happened so quick they didn't rightly know how it begun, only how it come out. What is sure is there was a bunch of shots, and when everbody had got around that bend Morton and Baker was both dead, and McCluskie was being drug over the rocks by his horse with his boot tangled in the stirrup. When they caught up with the horse McCluskie was bad off and didn't live but a few minutes. You hear different versions of this yet, including where the bodies was buried—depends on who's doing the telling. The Murphy-Dolan folks say they was all executed, with the Kid taking the lead. Our side has it that Morton made a grab for McCluskie's gun and got hold of it, but the Kid knocked him out of the saddle with a pistol shot, and then everybody commenced firing. Me? What I know is what the Kid said to me later, when we was over to San Patricio after the big shootout. He says, 'George, you know I never meant them birds to see Lincoln again.' Now, you can make of that what you want.

*

So now we was avenged, an eye for an eye, as the Bible has it. But that ain't the way these things almost always goes, least-ways, not then in Lincoln County. Soon as word got back about Morton and Baker, Sheriff Brady put a price on the Kid's head and Dick Brewer's, and ever other man that had gone after his possemen: Fred Waite, Doc Scurlock, Hendry Brown, Frank McNabb, Middleton, Charlie Bowdre, Jim French. Frank and me didn't go out, and so we wasn't wanted yet, but was soon to be. But these wanted men was now lawmen themselves, on account of McSween had figured a way to get around the sheriff and have a justice of the peace make Dick Brewer a special constable who had the power to collect a posse and go after the others who had been in on the killing of Tunstall. So now for the first time you had two rivaling gangs of lawmen, riding around after one another. It would have been funny if you wasn't part of it, but if you was, you knew both gangs wasn't out to make no arrests. They was hunting to the death.

Then you had the Kid. He was never bothered by the law and its paper and badges. He seen what become of Tunstall, and that was enough for him. It hit him some place that counted, wherever that was. He stayed friendly with us, still laughed and so forth, but I think he was pards with us so long as he could see we was useful to him in getting Tunstall's killers—and not just Morton and Baker. If we hadn't been useful, why, I believe he would have continued on his own way, hunting the bastards down, one at a time, till he finished the job, or until his luck run out and they fixed him first. Hard to make up your mind about an hombre set up so, ain't it? You could try sizing him up real quick and say, 'This here feller is just *loyal* clear through.' Or you might say to yourself, 'There's got to be some difference between a man and a killer dog like that Willard I had up on the Sugarite.' Long as I fed Willard and kept out of his way, he went after them cows. But get between him and his targets, and you'd be like that bull of Ernest's, missing your nuts.

I'm talking here as a man has had time to think back on these matters, time to think back on the Kid, and I have to say that back then I never would have thought to compare him to a killer dog—and I ain't necessarily doing so now. It makes you think, though, when you know that no matter *what*, a man ain't going to quit till his enemies is *all* dead. I don't know how many of us has got that kind of sand, or whatever it may be, in us. Maybe some of these famous gunmen—Clay Allison, Harden, Wild Bill—was built that way, I can't say. Of them I knew, wasn't none of them like that. Frank McNabb and Jack Middleton come closest, but not truly that close. McNabb was handy with a gun and quiet of manner. He had been a stock detective before he come into the territory, and though he never said this, I believe he had killed a man or two in that line of work. Jack Middleton was no doubt the savagest-looking desperado you ever seen, just the complete opposite to the Kid in that way. If you wasn't scared when you run across Jack Middleton, you wasn't paying good attention. And he could back it up: good shot, kept his head, was always ready to ride. Neither one was a match for the Kid. You could feel the difference between McNabb and the Kid that winter we bunked together. I can't put my finger on it, except to say that the Kid was readier to laugh than McNabb but was more serious some way than him, and I believe Frank himself seen that. Same with Middleton. Jack looked rough and was rough, but Jack liked to raise hell, when it could be done, which the Kid didn't. Jack liked his liquor, where the Kid almost never took a drink, only a glass of Juan Patron's beer when in Lincoln. Jack liked chasing tail, which the Kid was kind of an expert at, except that tail chased him, and so there wasn't no effort to it. But you know what Jack done after the fighting was over? He was a wanted man then, same as the rest of us, but one day without saying a word to any of us, he just rode off by himself into Kansas and some quiet little town where he run a store. Fact. Far as I know, he's up there yet, though of course by now he might be the cause of the grass growing greener over his final spot. Fred Waite done pret' near the same sort of thing. Frank McNabb, we'll never know what he might have turned to: there's some that once they get into the habit of making their way in the world with their gun, they don't seem able to do otherwise, even if offered—Hendry Brown was that way—, but Frank was killed early on in the war, so we'll never know.

Well, as I say, the Kid was sand all the way through, but now I wonder if that's the truly right way to size him up. Sand is grit, and he had it, all right. But still, as I think back on it, I find it don't quite get there somehow. Lots has got sand, some more than others, but he was just . . . different. You and me, folks can size us up, one way and another: 'Old man Coe, he's this and he's that, and he done some bad things when a young man, but now he's on the straight and narrer, and, take him all around, he ain't that bad a feller.' Same with you, if you see what I mean: you're a bit of this and a bit of that, and some cares for you, while others don't. But after you've said the Kid was cool when it was hottest, that the Kid was a randy rooster and a damn fine shot—when you say all that, you *still* ain't got him some way. There's something missing there. Maybe, when you add up all the things he was, you look at what you got, and it adds up wrong. So, you try again, adding it up, and it's still wrong, and it will *always* come out wrong. It's like it don't have an answer, like a zero. Maybe *way* down in him, where you'd been thinking he was sand, there ain't any sand, there ain't anything at all. Maybe that's what you saw in his eyes, that nothing.

Well, I don't know. But I do know this: us Regulators was goddamn happy he was riding amongst us instead of on the other side, and when he said he was going to do something—whatever it was—I don't recollect any of us crossing him. Might have been better all around if we had, because shortly after the Morton and Baker thing he said he had a plan to kill the sheriff.

*

That's a hell of a thing to plan to do, but it didn't seem to bother him none at all. All he said was that now that Morton and Baker was dead, Brady come next. He told the boys he knew Brady's morning routine, how he'd come down the street from his office at the Firm's store, walk past Tunstall's new store to take breakfast with his deputies, then walk back up, passing Tunstall's store again. The plan was to slip into town at night, hide out in the corral next to Tunstall's store, and fire on Brady when he come by after breakfast. Who was with him on this? he said, and Dash Waite and McNabb and Middleton right away said they was. He couldn't have picked out a better bunch. Frank and me was over on our places trying to keep up with our farms, which I was goddamn glad of, once I heard what was planned. I don't know what I would have said if asked: killing a sheriff is just a different deal, one of them things that made the war into a something nobody could have figured on—like a little old flame in a field that you stomp out with your heel, and the next thing you know it's flared up into a blaze that you got all around you, and you wonder how to get the hell out of there.

Even if McSween wanted nothing to do with murders and the like, it would have been impossible for him not to of known that the Kid and his bunch was hiding out in his corral: it was attached to his house. What the Kid might have told him when he slipped into town that night, I don't know; maybe he told him he was there to protect him, and by that point even a God-fearing lawyer like McSween would have seen that this was going to be a fight to the finish. Besides, he had a wife to consider. But whatever was said, and whatever McSween made of it, he found out quick the next morning what the Kid was up to when Brady and his men come by, likely picking their teeth and with their bellies satisfied—*ka-BLAM!*

When he was building the store, Tunstall was building it like a fort, as Frank seen, and in that corral wall there was gun ports, which the Kid and the others used to train their rifles. They hit Brady with a bunch of bullets and his deputy George Hindman—he had been in on the Tunstall thing—with some more. Billy Matthews got hit, but not too bad, and him and the other deputy, Dad Peppin, run off. Brady was killed before he hit the dust, but somehow he still got up and looked around him like he had dropped his toothpick, but then went down for good. Hindman was fatally shot in the belly. Then the Kid run out to collect a fine-looking Winchester Brady had, and Matthews shot from cover and hit him in the thigh. The other casualty was Squire Wilson, who had been hoeing his cabbages and took a stray bullet in the ass. All this took maybe two minutes. And so there you had the town sheriff laying dead in the main street. There was Deputy Hindman a-thrashing about and screaming for someone to help him, and Ike Stockton, who run a saloon, come out there and tried to drag him to cover, but then somebody put another bullet in him. Ike seen then it was no use and dropped him and run back in the saloon. Across the road, there was Squire Wilson, rolling about in his cabbage patch. And then

44

there was the Kid being helped into the saddle and the whole bunch riding down across the Bonito on their way out of town. Two minutes. But the outcome went on a long time afterwards, and was plenty bad for our side, on account of popular opinion changing right then.

When folks seen what happened to Tunstall they turned against the Firm—lot of 'em, anyways, that hadn't got caught up in the mess to that point. But this here, the dry-gulching of the sheriff and his deputies in broad daylight on the main street, that swung things back the other way. Folks begun figuring there wasn't *nothing* safe in Lincoln no more, not their wives, nor their children, nor their homes and businesses. Even if you wasn't to that point sided-up, you could get plugged like the squire, who turned out crippled for life, just on account of being outdoors hoeing his cabbages. So, quite a few folks said, "Fuck 'em both," and begun to look around for someone—*anyone*, really—to come in here and clean this up before the town and the whole county went back to the Indians. Some turned to Squire Wilson, banged up though he was, and he sent a messenger over to the fort to get Dudley to come on and establish civilization, in a manner of speaking. Then, he wrote up to Governor Axtell in Santa Fe, saying, help. So, though the Kid done what he set out to do, getting two more of Tunstall's killers, the outcome for us was bad. I don't think he ever gave a thought to that, on account of he was never really on either side.

Dudley didn't come; I guess he figured it wasn't the army's business. But Axtell did, to try to figure out what in the Sam Hill was happening to Tom Catron's investments. He gets down here and has got a dead sheriff on his hands and a replacement, John Copeland, who was a good friend of McSween. He's got a drunk, Murphy, wouldn't know a potato from a road apple, and another feller, who don't know nothing but fighting—that would be Jimmie Dolan. He's got the Firm's books, which is like a big knot that Winn Rigney left behind when he hightailed it back to Hondo in the night. And he's got us, the Regulators, with this killer boy leading them and like to ruin the Ring's entire scheme for the county.

So, he acted quick: fired Copeland and put in Dad Peppin. Fired the justice of the peace who give Dick Brewer his badge as Special Constable and canceled all his paper, and had Peppin write new papers naming Brewer and many of the Regulators outlaws. When we heard all this we figured Axtell had drawn up a new list of the citizens in the county and we wasn't anywhere on it: we had been changed from farmers or ranchers or cow-punchers into something you would hunt down and kill, like wolves or coyotes that was killing your lambs. But such was the high feeling by this point that all this did was make us more set than ever on hunting down our enemies before they could crack down on us. It wasn't no more than three or four days later that we found what we was looking for at Blazer's Mill.

*

We got word that an enemy posse had been spotted near Rin-coñada Canyon off the edge of the Mescalero reservation, which wasn't even in the county, but no matter, and we held a meeting about this next morning at my place. There was me and Frank, Dick Brewer, Charlie Bowdre, Fred Waite, Jack Middleton, and Frank McNabb. The Kid was over at San Patricio, getting his leg seen to, and Erasmo Chavez brought us word he would make it over if he was able. Well we wasn't about to go to war without him, wounded or not, but while having our breakfast we made out a plan, which was to ride up the Ruidoso, drop down through the reservation, and fetch up at Doc Blazer's to find out what he knew about that posse's movements. When we had talked through this, we sat around smoking, seeing to our weapons, and waiting on the Kid.

What had started out with a lot of low clouds now broke open and sunny around ten, and shortly after, here comes the Kid on a great big roan we never seen before, and you would certainly notice a horse like that, big as he was. And, my, how that roan could run! We found that out later, though now the Kid had him at an easy lope down the trail to the river, then reined him in to cross. It's funny how sharp my recollections was that day and how sharp they has stayed through all the years since, like there was a something telling me to be specially on the lookout, that something special was going to happen. This same feeling has come over me three other times in my life, and ever time that hunch has turned out true. Just now, talking to you this way, I still have a picture in my mind of the Kid as he looked on that sunny morning, splashing across the river on the roan, wearing that sugarloaf hat, and then coming on up to where we waited. When he got off his horse, he did so ginger, favoring that leg, you see. Up close, he didn't look so good, kind of peakéd like, but when Dick told him the program he just nodded and said he wouldn't want to miss the fun.

Off we went then, upstream, and we didn't spot nothing till we got onto the reservation. Handsome country there, all pines and a good many creeks and ponds. Then we spotted a bunch of Indians through the trees, but when they seen us with our weapons and all, they left off whatever they was up to and run off. It was well past noon when we come out of the timber and looked down to see the blue smoke curling out of Doc Blazer's chimney, and Dick said, 'Boys, I'm set for a plateful of Mrs. Godfroy's dinner.' Mrs. Godfroy was well known up that way as a good cook, someone you would ride out of your way for. That cheered us some, where before we had been pretty quiet—tense, I guess, as you will be when you're hunting trouble. We followed the creek down the ravine, and Doc Blazer seen us and come out, waving his hat. 'Boys,' he hollered, 'you're in luck! Mrs.

Godfroy has a fresh-made mess of turkey hash just waiting on you. I'll see to your horses, and welcome.' So, we went in happy, all but Dick, who wanted to talk to Blazer, and Frank and Jack Middleton, who was posted as guards.

Blazer was a dentist by trade, but them days a man with such training would be called upon to do any number of things, from setting bones to treating gunshot wounds to birthing babies. The word 'sawbones' fit Blazer, on account of he done a good bit of that. He also run what you might call a roadhouse, a big old barn of a place where you could get a meal and have your horse tended to. Down below that, where the creek run, he had a sawmill. Take it all around, I think he must have been doing fairly well for himself. While we all sat down at a long plank table, he was telling Dick that a Peppin posse had nooned there the day before and had showed him brand-new warrants naming Dick and the Kid as wanted for the murder of Brady and Hindman. Afterwards, they had ridden up into the reservation, and Blazer thought they might pick up our trail there and double back this way. While we was discussing this development, Frank come in quick and says, 'Boys, there's a man down to the mill, riding this way, and he's heavy-armed." We judged this might possibly be the lead man from the Peppin posse, though he wasn't coming from the right direction. Whatever the case, we jammed home another bite and then begun to buckle up. I went out on the porch to join Frank, and there below on the far side of the creek we seen who it was—Buckshot Roberts on a bay mule, wearing two pistols, a cartridge belt across his chest, and a rifle resting on the pommel. He was just sitting there, looking up steady at us. Frank and him knew each other and had once been on fair terms, though Roberts wasn't a friendly sort: he had been shot up bad in the Civil War, was full of lead here and there, so they said, and had a game leg. Carrying all that around ever day might make any man onrey. Frank signed him, raising his hand slow.

'Howdy, Roberts.' Old Buckshot nodded a little and just sat on that mule. 'Son,' Frank says to me, keeping his eye on Roberts, 'go back in there and tell the boys it's Buckshot Roberts down here, and he appears to be loaded for trouble.'

There was two windows in the mess hall, and after I reported what Frank said we all crowded up there and looked down to where Frank had gone down into the yard to wait while Roberts come across the creek and then up to Frank and got down, slow and stiff—stumpy feller with that game leg bent and leaning on his rifle, which we seen was a Yeller Boy; called it that on account of it had a brass magazine and butt and was a real popular gun them days—still is, if you can find one. Well, they commenced talking, and we could see Roberts shake his head a time or two and dig that brass butt into the dirt, like he was fixing to screw himself into the ground with it, and after a bit Frank, he shook his head and turned to come up to the building. And there was old Buckshot, down there alone in the yard, and he ain't even looking around after Frank—just stood there, leaning on his Yeller Boy and awaiting whatever would come. I can picture him so even yet.

Frank told us he had explained the condition to Roberts: that he had done stuck his pecker in a hornet's nest, that there was eight armed men up there that was on the hunt for them that killed Tunstall, which included him, Buckshot. Roberts said that was funny, because here he was with warrants in his saddlebags for the killers of Brady and Hindman, and that he made no doubt that Dick Brewer, Charlie Bowdre, and what he called 'that little cur, Kid Antrim,' was up there in the building, and if they was, he was bound to serve them warrants, no matter who else might be along. Frank didn't say nothing to Roberts on that particular score, just pointed out the condition and said he personally would guarantee Roberts wouldn't be harmed if he would surrender but would be safely jailed at Lincoln.

49

When Frank had finished there was some high talk amongst us, with some saying Roberts was nothing but a murderer, same as Morton and Baker and Tom Hill; that it was just his tough luck to run into our bunch; and if things was different, they was satisfied he would shoot his prisoners down before they ever got to jail—including Dick, who wasn't even involved—just to collect his reward. Then there was some talk against Frank, too, who they said wasn't deputized to offer Roberts a damn thing. But right there Doc Blazer, bless him, got into it. Said, let him go down and talk to Roberts, which he done, and we all crowded up to the windows again to watch. It was the same as with Frank— Doc Blazer pointing up to where we was, and Buckshot shaking his head and trifling with the Yeller Boy. Finally, when he turned and spat and pointed to the mule with its saddlebags, Blazer seen it was no use, that Roberts was set on serving them warrants.

Now, just *how* he figured on doing that—well, what would *you* think? I mean, here you got eight armed men that had come looking for the enemy, and you're one man down there in the yard with your pistols, your rifle, and them warrants. Seems kind of hopeless, don't it? But I'll tell you, when Doc Blazer told us how matters was and how Roberts cursed us all, well, the reaction was remarkable. It give us all a thought, because a man in that condition, he ain't got nothing more to lose, in a manner of speaking—he's already a dead man and knows it. But then, *you* got to figure you might lose your own life while he's losing his: he's going to stand there and work that lever-action till he goes down—and maybe even a bit after that—and who knows where all them bullets is likely to land? So, when Dick says, who'll volunteer to take him? why, there was this hesitation amongst us who was all thinking the same thing: we're going to go down there and put all kinds of holes in this crazy fucker, but do I want him to dust *me* while we're at it? But it was just that one moment, and the Kid, who had been sitting down on account of his leg, he stands up and tells Dick, 'You can send me, Dick, though I ain't a cur.' And right quick Charlie Bowdre and Middleton come in, and then I kind of like heard myself saying the same, and Dick points to us and then to himself and says, 'That makes five, and we got more if needed.'

I checked my rifle and cleared my pistol from the holster in case the riding had jammed it down some, and then we went out along the porch, which was all in shadow, and then around the corner into the sun, and I recall how hot and bright and yeller everything looked just then when we rounded on old Buckshot. There he stood, foursquare and facing us so as to give us a good target. He brought up the Yeller Boy, waist-level and deliberate, and fired, hitting Middleton in the chest high up, right when Charlie Bowdre got off a shot hit him in the stomach, and I seen the dust fly out of Buckshot's shirt in a gray little puff. Even so, he never give an inch, just worked that lever, and his next shot hit Charlie's belt buckle, and his cartridge belt flang off with a *whap* and landed on my boot, and I was raising my rifle, but didn't have it no more. It was like it had flown away somewheres like Charlie's cartridge belt. Just then there come a hot buzzing up my arm, as though a swarm of bees had got into it, and I looked down, and my hand was so shiny it hurt me to look at it, and the buzzing was now so loud I couldn't even hear the *blam! blam! blam!* all around me, and it come over me that I had been hit.

Well, I commenced to run, not away from Roberts but straight across his line of fire—don't ask me why I done so, I just done it. Come near to costing me my life, though it wasn't until a few days later that I come to that understanding when one of the boys, Doc Scurlock, was looking after me and says, 'George, what's this all about?' holding me by my shirt front. I looked to where he had hold of me, and, by Godfrey, there was a bullet hole through it and my vest as well: when I had run right past Roberts he had naturally fired on me but missed. Another inch and I'd still be up there at Blazer's Mill right this minute instead of sitting here telling you about it.

As it was, I made it around the building, old Buckshot being occupied elsewhere, and got on the porch, and I looked down at the planks, sort of wondering why they was getting bigger and bigger. Course they wasn't at all; it was me falling down towards them. Next thing I knew, there was Doc Blazer kneeling beside me and saying, 'Oh, well! Oh, well!' or some such. He was swabbing my hand with whiskey and then wrapping it tight with some flour sacking that Mrs. Godfroy used as towels. Then he helped get me propped against the building and set the jug next to me. 'Here, Coe,' he says, 'you're going to need this.' Then he run back in the building. I got hold of the jug with my good hand and had a real pull, but it didn't stay with me long, as it come right back up along with Mrs. Godfroy's hash, so there I was, a real mess and couldn't do nothing about it but just sprawl there in my blood and puke and hear all the shooting and shouting.

But then it suddenly quit, and some of the boys piled around the corner, including Frank, who come over and helped me up, and we went in after the rest. Inside, there was so much hollering I couldn't make nothing of it, except I seen Middleton, blood all down his shirtfront and him crouched in the corner with his teeth bared like an animal that has been bayed. And I seen Charlie Bowdre all bent down and holding his guts like he had a mighty bellyache, which he did. And there was the Kid looking at his sleeve, which had blood on it. But none of these was the cause of the hullabaloo. It turned out that after all them first shots was exchanged everbody sort of scattered. Dick and Fred Waite run downhill to the creek where the cover was better. Some others tried to get behind some truck there in the yard or under a wagon. Buckshot had got himself inside a lean-to at the far end of the building, and bad hit as he was with Bowdre's bullet through his belly, he drug a mattress off a cot and propped it in the doorway and got down behind it to continue his shooting. The ones with the best angle on him was Dick and Fred down below, and they kept firing at the lean-to, figuring they'd shoot hell out of it and was bound to hit Roberts again, by and by. Dick was firing from behind a pile of sawlogs, and Roberts seen just where he was, and so the next time Dick poked his head up to aim Roberts was fixed on the spot and blew his left eye out—killed him dead instantly. Hell of a shot and would have been so for a well man let alone a gut-shot feller that was dying.

Way later—, this was after the World War—, I went over to Blazer's Mill to pay a call on Doc Blazer. We was good friends on account of his saving my hand but hadn't seen one another in some time. Place was pret' near the same, though they no longer run the roadhouse. But we got to talking about that hellacious day and Buckshot's killing of Dick, and so we went out to where the lean-to had once been, and Doc paced off the distance down to where Dick had been hiding behind them sawlogs, and he made it one hundred twenty-five yards. 'Course Roberts was helped some by firing downhill where there wasn't so much drop to his bullet as would have been the case firing up the other way. Still, it was remarkable.

While we was looking around down there I asked Doc where they buried poor old Dick; I had heard one thing and another, including that they never buried him at all until some time later, when his people got up the nerve to come and gather up what was left of him and take him back to the ranch. Doc shook his head, no. Said he wasn't certain of the exact spot but that his sawmill boss, Tom Patton, had knocked together a big long box out of some scrap lumber and put both Dick and Buckshot in it together and buried it. Ain't that a hell of a note, though—waiting for Judgment Day, jammed up next to the man that killed you?

Well, sir, that was what had the boys hollering so up in the mess hall, and some was for rushing the lean-to. And some said it was that kind of angry behavior got Dick killed. And some was for burning the old fucker out—which wouldn't have made Doc Blazer too happy, the lean-to being attached to the building. But here again, Doc finally got things simmered down just enough to say he would try to get a word with Roberts, that Roberts looked mighty bad hit, and if he was, then there wouldn't be no point in risking more death by further action. And that's what he done, though it was a dangerous thing to try; you don't know what a man's likely to do that is armed and dying. But Doc stuck his head out the mess hall window and hollered down to the lean-to. Said, 'Roberts, I'm Doctor Blazer. Let me see to you.' There was a long silence then, but finally Roberts come back, 'Ain't no use. I am killed.'

'Well, let me see to you, still,' Doc said. 'It may be I can ease your pain some.'

There was some more silence, and then Roberts kind of grunted and said, 'Well, goddamn it, come ahead then,' but said, 'Come alone. Anybody else with you, I'll put a window in you both.' He was a game feller, you got to give him that.

So Doc went the long way around the building to the lean-to and was gone quite a spell, and while he was we looked around the mess hall and seen we was a sorry bunch. Jack Middleton had a wound up near the shoulder and was still gritting his teeth over in the corner. The Kid had a flesh wound in his arm. Charlie Bowdre was still crippled up with his bellyache. And there was me who had a hand tore up from the same bullet. Meanwhile, down there behind them logs was our chief with a hole in his head. And all this was done by that one man working his Yeller Boy down in the yard, but we wasn't in no mood to heroize him none.

Finally, here come Doc Blazer, who said, 'Boys, best to leave him be: he can't last an hour. But he still has his guns, and it might be costly yet to rush him. I'd not even wait him out, on account of while you was, that Peppin bunch might just come down the ravine on you, and then you'd have another fight on your hands.' Then he got busy with our wounded and finally got around to me.

'Coe,' he says, 'I may be able to save your finger at the knuckle, but the top half will have to come off. And if I take off this bit of flesh on your thumb, I believe I can stitch it up. Let me go for my kit.'

Presently, he come back with it and had Frank and Fred Waite hold me down and give me this thin bar of scrap iron from the mill to bite down on. Then he sawed off this end of the finger and patched up the thumb, washed 'em both good with diluted carbolic acid, and stitched them up with thread made of cattle gut—done it all right there on the mess table with the boys look-ing on. It was a first-rate job, too. I have a professional judgment on that on account of just last year there come a feller with his wife and kiddies down to my stand, and he was a sure-enough doctor from some big-time hospital, way up in Minnesota. We got to talking about this and that while the wife looked through the pictures, and he asked me if I had lost part of my finger in a farming accident, and so I told him the story. He examined Doc Blazer's handiwork and said he would like to see the missing part, so I brung him up here—same as you—and got the jar down. He turned it around real careful but didn't say nothing. Then, when he was taking his leave, he says, 'That's a remarkable job. You're a lucky man.' He was right about that, sure. The wife and kiddies didn't want to see any of this; they waited down by the stand. But he was right interested.

*

Banged up like I was, I was scared to go back to my place, where I would be easy pickings for an enemy posse, plus me and Frank was now outlaws on account of the killing of Buckshot Roberts, who was legally a lawman carrying warrants. Then the Kid told

55

us he was going back to San Patricio to heal up and why didn't we think of coming along with him, which is what we concluded to do. This meant we had to leave our places with nobody living on them, though we was able to get Erasmo Chavez or his cousin to check on them once in a while. Meanwhile, both Lou and Al Coe had already hauled up stakes to get away from all of this. They first went up to Romeroville and then ended up back where they started, on the Sugarite. So, this left us with everthing we had been working towards open to the wind, so to speak, and the county lawless. But wasn't a thing we could do about it.

*

San Patricio was cozy them days, sweet really, snugged up next to the mountains with the river running through it and orchards, shade trees, and pasture lands. They had them two cantinas and a new-built church for the new padre who had scared the fun out of the young gals, name of Herlihey. I never did see much of him because the Kid had us holed up on the far side of the river with a family named Jaramillo that was big in the village. Rolando Jaramillo was the *mayor domo*—that's the water chief, a very important position. He had a fine place and a casita where he put us. It was quite small, but if we didn't move around too much, we could fit into it all right. There was a bridge over the river to get to it, and Rolando always had someone posted there to see no strangers come across. The padre never come over, nor many that wasn't family, except on errands.

At first, we didn't feel like doing much of anything. Frank was bitter on account of having to be away from his place but was good about washing my hand ever day with a bottle of the carbolic acid Doc Blazer give him. The Kid's thigh wound was still troublesome, though the wound Roberts give him wasn't no more than a scratch. Me, I didn't do nothing but sit out there in the orchard back of the casita with my elbow on a table and my hand up in the air. Somehow, it felt better that way, but I don't mind saying this particular time wasn't a string of Sunday school picnics for me. Frank would sit out there with me some, the Kid less, and once in a while all three of us. Frank was finding it hard to get his mind off his place and our mowing machine, which was just sitting up in a field where it might be shot to pieces by our enemies, and one day when us three was out there talking he said tomorrow he was determined to ride over there to have a look. But the Kid told him one man riding over there wasn't going to change a thing, and that when he—the Kid, that is— got to where riding was comfortable, if Frank was still so set on going, he would go with him. Other than this sort of thing, there wasn't nothing to do but sit around, smoke, and wait till we felt better, which seemed a real long time in arriving.

Meanwhile, the news of the war come to us regular from along the river, and the news wasn't good—hadn't been since the Brady killing, which was like a bloodstain for our side that wouldn't wash off. And then it got more gloomish yet with word of a sizeable shootout near the old Fritz ranch. That was where Frank McNabb got shot off his horse and was chased down and murdered by a bunch led by Peppin. McNabb was one of our best, worth two or three other fighters, and his loss was a stinger, but the Kid didn't say nothing about it, except that Peppin needed killing, and that when he got healed up, he would see to it. The Firm, he said, was bound to run short of sheriffs at some point, but for now we had to lay low and wait for the right time. Me and Frank didn't say nothing to this, but I recollect at the time thinking that making a sideline of dry-gulching sheriffs seemed kind of disastrous.

*

This was a time when me and Frank got a steady look at the Kid, more so even than that winter he bunked with me, because he was with us ever day, and, I tell you, it was a real education to see how popular he was with the Mexicans, especially the gals who come across the bridge late afternoons, bringing fresh laundry and all kinds of food. They had to take turns shaving him and combing his hair and singing to him while he sat there with his stocking feet propped up, smiling a bit—but careful-like—to show he appreciated the attention. And even though they took turns singing and shaving him, there still wasn't enough of El Chivato to go around, and that's a natural fact. As for his bunkmates, me and Frank was near invisible.

When the village would have their *bailes* the three of us might go over for a look, just to break up the sameness, but the Kid didn't do no dancing on account of his leg, and I didn't want to move this hand around more than strictly necessary. Frank was all right with a woman long as he was paying for it, but he wasn't comfortable asking any of them Mex gals to dance. He was always somehow shy that way, and never did marry. Along with the dancing they had regular monte games going in them cantinas, but the Kid didn't do none of that neither, good a player as he was. Frank asked him once did he miss playing, and why didn't he? The Kid said if he played some and happened to win, this being a small place, it might not sit so good, and the way things was going with the war we was going to need all the friends we could gather.

Things run along like this well into summer. The Kid healed up good and went back to dancing and staying away nights, though he still didn't play monte. At daybreak he'd come across the river, and we would hear him sliding into bed. Then he'd sleep late, get up for a cold cup of coffee and yesterday's tortilla and then pad down to see to his horse. When that roan spotted him through the trees, he'd come a-snorting at a hard trot right to the fence and then foller the Kid along it just like a dog. The Kid could make it back, turn, trot off, come back, just by making motions with his head or his hand. It was a sight to see.

Then there come a day when he told me that if I didn't start to learning to shoot left-handed, I was certain to be killed quick once we was forced to break cover, which we was going to have to do. 'You're a wanted man now, George,' he said, 'and we can't stay holed up here forever.' I knew he was right soon as he spoke and had been thinking this way a bit myself, but had been trying to put it out of my mind the way you will when you got something that's big trouble and don't appear to have no way around it. I said did he think he would teach me, and he said, no—only way was for me to practice. That next day him and me went over to a bean field beyond where our horses was, and the Kid set up some bottles. We begun snapping at them, and at first it was right awkward for me, but not so much as I had feared, on account of I was always a little both-handed: I was right-handed, yes, but when I reached for things, I always reached with my left, and if I had something to do such as tying a knot or buckling a harness strap, why, I used my left for such work. Now, after all these years this way my left hand is a good deal stronger than my natural one, but I believe it might have been that way even then. So, pulling a pistol trigger wasn't too bad once I begun to get the feel for it. What was tough was learning to sight a rifle with my left eye: I kept on switching back and forth between eyes, trying to get things lined up proper, and I missed quite a few shots I might have made before, but I kept at it steady: a man will be encouraged that way if he thinks his life might depend on it. I didn't get to be a crack shot left-handed, but then, I never had truly been that right-handed. But at least now I wasn't a sitting duck, neither, and begun to judge I could crack down on a man with some prospect of hitting him, especially with a pistol—enough so, anyways, to make him take me into his calculations. This was soon enough to be a necessity, mostly because of the bad way things continued to go with the war: there was that shootout at the Fritz ranch that cost us Frank McNabb;

there was Dad Peppin, who turned out to be a harder man than Brady; and there was Peppin's new reinforcements sent down by the Santa Fe Ring. And there was another thing as well that begun to make our life at San Patricio different, something I got myself into in the village.

Name was Nazarina. She was cousin to Manuela Bowdre, Charlie's wife, and was one of them that waited on the Kid. She didn't do much for him that I could see, only stood by and watched while her older sister and the others saw to him. But— well, you'll notice things about a gal when you ain't got one of your own. So, I noticed her hair, which she had slicked back and tied with a ribbon and was always clean-looking like she'd been in the river before she come across the bridge. And when you ain't feeling like a top hand yourself them kind of things'll win you. Frank and me had one favorite cantina on account of Erasmo and never even went in the other one, but some way I got the strong notion she might be working over there, and sure enough, one night when I talked Frank into going to the other place, just for the change, there she was, wiping down the tables and bringing the drinks.

These wasn't rough places like the hog ranches, not that Mexes ain't ever rowdy—they are. But San Patricio was so small it seemed like someway everbody was hooked onto everbody else, and so it wasn't like the hog ranches where you was in a roomful of strangers you didn't care if you ever saw again. Now, through the Bible, I've come to learn we are all hooked together some way, even if not by blood, which causes me to think back on these days I'm telling about when we was hunting one another just like the animals in the jungle. I never seen the like in San Patricio, which don't mean it didn't go on, only that if there was blood feuds like you hear of, I missed it. Probably missed a great deal on account of our setup across the river but also because, after all, I was a white man from upriver who didn't know nobody, and they didn't know me from Adam's off-ox. But I wanted to get to know Nazarina, all right, and finally I managed that.

After her work, we'd walk along the river through the trees in the general direction of her home, though we wasn't in any especial hurry to reach there. She didn't have no English, so most of our talking was signs and a few Mexican words I knew, but we got across to each other good. That time of year the grass by the river was yet sweet-smelling and soft, and after a little bit we would get down on it. It had been a spell for me, and I hadn't had even my own hand on my pecker, not being both-handed that way and the right hand being so touchy it would have been a good deal more hurtful than a pleasure. Nazarina was like the grass, and I'll tell you, that gal had some thrust to her.

One night we're down there amongst the trees, just going to town, when all of a sudden I heard something and—*quick*—I jerked away, but she held on tight and rolled over atop me. Then I made out what it was: that goddamn roan snorting across the pasture towards us, and just as I'm about to curse him for his interference, she claps a hand hard over my mouth, and we hold quiet. There was someone close by, coming along through the trees, and he's coming along real slow. There wasn't much moon, and anyway, I couldn't have seen nothing with Nazarina atop me and her hand over my face and holding me down in the grass. Then I heard the roan whicker, low and friendly, and I knew who it was, at which point Nazarina wouldn't have had to hold me still no more, for I understood the terrible danger we both was in. If we had moved a grass spear, the Kid would have whipped that .41 Thunderer out like lightning itself, and that would have been the end for me and her both.

Well, he went on past, going slow and quiet, like he might have been in his stocking feet, as often he was around the casita. But we stayed right where we was, having no way to judge where he might be and the roan having quieted. Seemed like he was gone a long time, but then, in that condition it naturally would. Nazarina never moved other than to take her hand from my mouth. Then we heard him again, coming back through the trees, slow and light-footed, and when he had passed by and been gone a good while, she got up, still listening and then signed me to stay where I was and went on back towards the village. I got up, adjusted my clothing and dusted myself off, wondering what in the Sam Hill all this meant. A man don't often get shoved around by his girlfriend and told to stay put, especially where it's a white man and a Mex gal, and considerably younger at that. If things had been different, I would have been riled, I guess, but my pride or whatever it was was still tamped down by knowing how close we come to death with the sound of the Kid going by like a mountain cat bearing down on its target. And so I had to carry all that back to Jaramillo's casita, where Frank was already turned in and the Kid gone off elsewhere. I wanted like anything to wake Frank and talk this over, him being more level-headed than me, but I didn't.

That was one restless night, I can tell you, and the next morning as well, wondering what the Kid had been up to out there in the night and what to say about it to Frank. Maybe all it was was him just seeing to his horse. He set great store by it, that was certain, and even though he stole a good many horses in his time and rode some of them quite a bit before selling or trading them, he kept this one until Garrett cornered him and the others at Stinking Springs and took it from him. Maybe he done this way ever night, I thought—except me and her had been going down there regular and never heard nothing but owls and coyotes. And then, how did Nazarina come to know soon as I did myself that it was him creeping along there? Or was she just worried that someone from the village would catch us at our fun?

You can appreciate that I had a deal to think about that afternoon when the Kid come out behind the casita and said why didn't we go and pop some bottles. That made me wish mighty hard I could think of a reason not to do that just then, but nothing would come to me on the jump-up, except another wish, which was that Frank hadn't gone over to the cantina for a glass of beer, something very unusual for him that time of day. So there was nothing for it but to go along, the Kid quiet but easy and me quiet and very uneasy, wondering even if I might be taking my last walk, and then at the same time telling myself this was foolishness—that there weren't any good reason to be thinking that way.

We never got to the bean field. When we come to the corral where our horses was and the roan come snorting up, the Kid laid his hand on him and then rolled a cigarette, and I done likewise, turning away just a bit so he couldn't see how unsteady my hands was. But he wasn't paying no attention to me whatever but was looking away into the distance and seemingly taking pleasure in his smoke.

'You know, George,' he says at last, 'this is some sweet place, ain't it? Snug, too. Anything happens here, it gets around pretty slick. So, the other day when I was paying Manuela a visit and asking after Charlie and them I heard something.' He puffed away and put his hand on the roan again, and I wondered whether that was it—that he wasn't going to say what he had heard. And what was I supposed to do then? But finally he went on, saying that under other conditions maybe this thing wouldn't take Manuela so hard, but that she knew we wasn't fixing to settle down here and become part of the village, and that her and Charlie would be mighty unhappy if we was suddenly to leave and have her young cousin left behind, and in a family way with no man to help her. I didn't know what to say to that, so we just went on smoking and looking away upriver with the minutes rolling by like they was boulders, till at last he looks over at me with them no-nerve eyes and says, 'Let's go pop some bottles,' which we done.

It didn't take no genius to get his drift, but the more I turned it around in my head, the more I couldn't seem to disentangle the message from the one who brung it. Manuela Bowdre was one fiery bitch—we all seen that—, and if she and Charlie had a hair up their hind end about me and Nazarina, well, maybe I could figure a way around that if I had to and could go on meeting up with her. If I couldn't, then that would be some tough titty, as they say.

But what if it was really the Kid that had the hair? I couldn't get it out of my head the way he sounded coming through the trees, and when I'd picture him those few feet off from us, I'd see him with his pistol out and ready to fire at a sound. The more I thought like this, the more it didn't seem like a man going out to say goodnight to his horse. I concluded I just had to talk this over with Frank that night when we was going over to our usual cantina, except when we got there I started right in on the whiskey like a dog at its water dish. Before I knew it I was drunked-up good. Frank, he sized me up and said, 'Son, we best get you back to the bunkhouse,' which he had some trouble doing, and then I went to bed without being able to say a word about what was so heavy on my mind.

The Kid didn't come back that night nor the next day, neither, and I wasn't going around hunting up his company. That night after supper I went across the bridge and brought back a bottle of whiskey and asked Frank to sit out with me and drink it as I was feeling poorly—which was no lie, what with the Kid on my mind and Nazarina bothering other parts of me. But just as I was starting in on what had happened down along the river, Frank opened up about what he'd been told that afternoon: a rough customer name of Selman had showed up at his place with a bunch of other hard cases and stopped Erasmo's cousin from threshing by taking off most of the horses. He would have taken the last team, only Tomás Chavez, the cousin, said they was his and begged them not to take them, and for some reason they didn't. Frank said it was clear Selman had been given information that we wasn't on our places, that they was undefended. So, instead of me talking about the Kid and Nazarina, that's what we talked about: how things was going from bad to worse for us and what we could do about it all. Frank said he wished he knew where the Kid had got to as he could generally be counted on to have an idea on how to handle big trouble, and this was sure enough trouble that could well end in our complete ruination.

His wish shortly come true that next morning when the Kid showed up with Erasmo, Tomás, and three or four other Mexicans, and then we all got together there in the orchard. After the Kid introduced us and we had swapped talk and had a smoke, he said these boys was parts of a bunch he'd gathered from the village and nearby, and that we was all to meet up with the rest of the Regulators and go over to Lincoln and have it out then and there with the Firm. The way he lined it out for us, since the Fritz ranch shootout where we lost McNabb, things had got more desperate than ever. Our side was now greatly outmanned and would be so at Lincoln, too. But maybe, if we was to slip into town at night, surprise might possibly turn the tables for us and give us a chance to finish off our enemies.

'It's come down to us against the Ring,' is how he put it. 'We can't sit here and wait for them to hunt us down like curs.' When he said that he smiled that careful little smile he had and moved his hands over the table, almost like he was laying out a deck of cards. He was ever a gambler, through and through, and this was his kind of game: us against the Ring, bucking the tiger. Nobody said a word then. Instead, we just set about gathering our things, making ready to meet up with the rest of the Regulators and then ride on to Lincoln in the night.

IV

We was sixty strong. Most was Mexicans the Kid and Erasmo Chavez had gathered up from along the river, from San Patricio but also Picacho, which had been persecuted considerable by the Firm on account of them folks was known to be friendly to Tunstall and the Kid. There was quite a number waiting for us in Lincoln, too; most was associated with Juan Patron and his family. Patron probably knew better than any the kind of people was in the Firm: they had murdered his pa and had shot Juan in the back, crippling him up for life; so, ever time he commenced to take a step he had a reason to recollect his enemies. Still, the heart of this whole thing was us Regulators—something we was to find out the hard way over the next five days. Before us, all these others hadn't done nothing about the Firm and likely never would have. I can't tell you just why that was. Some said Mexes was natural cowards. Some said it was that Santa Ana and them got licked back in forty-six, and that convinced all Mexicans they wasn't equal to the white man, and so had to take whatever was handed down. Some said it was the firepower the whites had, and others said numbers. Me, I say it might been a bit of all these, but what made the big difference was what the Firm had backing it, the Ring.

Now, you take a Mexican feller, working hard on his bit of land—wife, kiddies, maybe not that much good soil or reliable water—, and somehow he gets crosswise with his white neighbor and figures to go to the law, and he does. He finds out it's all white. And not only that, it ain't even the law, maybe, at least not *all* of the law. It's what some white man *tells* him is the law, and not the white man he's talking with, but some other white man, way off somewheres, somebody he can't set his eyes on and talk with, somebody he will *never* be able to talk with. So then, he does the only thing he can do. He rams his hands in his pockets and goes back home to his little place, his dusty house, and his wife and kids and his goats and chickens. And he doesn't say nothing further about it, just gets behind the plow again and hopes his white neighbor don't burn him out for trying to go to the law, because even if that was to happen, wouldn't be nothing he could do about that, neither. This condition goes on, father to son. But then, along comes the Kid and Martin Chavez with him, and they say to Luis or Antonio, 'Hey, we're fed up with this horseshit. We're gathering up men just like yourself, and we're riding in together to Lincoln, and we're going to show them fat bastards what the law really is.' Hellfire, you got a gun, a horse, and any guts behind your belt buckle, you *got* to join up, you know? And many of them did, some with guns wasn't worth a shit, maybe shot black powder, paper cartridges, took five minutes to reload and was more dangerous to the owner than the enemy. Yet they strapped up and joined us, though some was a good deal more useful than others. But if a man has a gun, you don't know if the goddamn thing works or not, or if the man behind it can work it or not. But unless you're a fool, you got to respect the man until he proves that ain't necessary.

*

We come together under darkness down on the Bonito beyond Ike Ellis's store. It was past midnight by the time we was all there, and not a dog had sent up an alarm, though when you get that many horses together they're bound to start talking to one another some. Martin Chavez must have done considerable scouting, maybe with help from Juan Patron, because it was him said, 'You go here,' and 'You go there.' He sent one party across the road and up along the slopes behind the Montaño store to where they had a good view of the Wortley Hotel and most of the upper part of town. Some others went up into the Torreon—that was a round tower built against the Indians by the settlers quite some years back; still there and an interesting structure if you ain't seen it. Another party was in the Tunstall store, another in the McSween house, and still another in a storehouse next door to that. At the beginning I was in the McSween house and Frank in the Torreon. Well before sunup we was all in place, just waiting for the enemy to show himself.

Inside the McSween house, except for the nervy jabber of Mrs. McSween and her sister and kids, it was quiet. The kiddies didn't know nothing, of course, and you could hardly blame the sisters for going on as they was: they knew they was trapped there and bound to stay until all was done, whenever that would be and however it turned out. We hardly seen anything of McSween himself. The house was built like a squared-off horseshoe with an ell connecting the two wings, and I believe he was in the west wing, behind the kitchen. Later, when it was all over, the Kid said he'd gone back there once or twice to see how he was holding up and said he was writing letters. Peculiar thing to be doing, but maybe he was saying his goodbyes.

After a bit, even the ladies hushed, and then for a spell wasn't nothing but the sun moving along the road and us watching it come on and then reaching in to where we waited, trying not to squeeze our rifles too tight but getting scratchy with the waiting. Then we seen movement up by the Montaño place, and inside there was sounds now, boys checking their weapons, a hammer being pulled back against its spring, somebody letting go a long breath like he'd been holding it in all night. But it turned out to be just a Mexican woman going slow across the road with a pail, and so then you had to relax back and resume waiting. The sun went on past us, roosters started up, and a couple of dogs, and just then come a *boom!* from a big gun—made us all jump—and that sound bounced around, up and down the road and off the hillsides, and while it was yet doing that there come a high scream—'*ai-eee!*'—like that. Later, we learned the big boom had been Alphonso Montoya, feller from Picacho, who had let go on someone coming out of the Wortley. Only gun I know that can make a racket like that is what Montoya had, a Sharps—one of them things that could knock a buffalo bull on his ass at six hundred yards you took him right. That was the last we heard out of that man and the first shot of the shootout. Following it, shots was fired from the Wortley and from the Firm's store, but we had got in the first lick, which the Kid had said we had to do in order to gain the quick upper hand and beat the odds.

It didn't turn out like that, though. After them first volleys where everybody was letting go because the feller next to you was doing the same, things simmered down quite a bit, like maybe everybody begun to think that a lot of this was just wasted powder and you maybe didn't have all the ammunition in the world, though it was true we had a pretty good supply from the Tunstall store. And who could tell how long this thing was going to go on? By the end of that first day the only casualty we knew of was that man Montoya dropped with his Sharps. Rest was aimless firing and name-calling, back and forth.

That day was when I got my first good look at our newest Regulator, name of Tom O'Folliard. How he come to be attached to us I've forgotten, but it was sometime after Blazer's Mill and might have been through Dash Waite—seems I heard it that way once. He wasn't Pat Garrett's length but was sure enough a long drink of water, and though thin was tough. I never did have much conversation with him, him being pretty close-mouthed, and what I did hear was mainly cuss words, like 'fuck,' which he said a good deal, and 'shit,' which appeared to be his next favorite, and these was kind of mumbled past a cigarette he had in his mouth all the time, whether it was going or not. Frank talked with him more and said he was an orphan whose natural parents was taken off with the smallpox down in Old Mexico and was raised by relations back in Uvalde, where the family was from. There was two things about him that made him useful: he was game, and he had fastened onto the Kid like a stray pup: follered him everwhere and would do whatever the Kid wanted done, whether that was seeing to his horse while the Kid went in to have a session with one of his señoritas, or riding point into some tricky spot where the Kid smelled trouble. Watching him that first day, I come to believe that if the Kid was to have said, 'Tom, stick your head out the window and draw some fire so we can see where it's coming from,' he would have done that. Loyalty is a great thing, on account if a man don't have it, you never know where you are with him. But, by Godfrey, you got to have some common sense alongside it, seems to me, and I don't know but old Tom might have been a tad short there. I say that because the next afternoon while we was hollering bad things across at the enemy—all about your mother and what your pa done with your sister—and firing once in a while when we thought we seen movement, there come one of the black troopers from the fort, riding hard through town with what was later learned to be a message from Dudley to Dad Peppin. When he larruped past us, O'Folliard took a shot at him—most likely on account of his color—but missed. Nobody said nothing about this at the time, but it turned out this was the cause of Dudley eventually coming into town with cavalry, infantry, a cannon, and a gatling gun that was said to shoot hundreds of bullets in a minute. Dudley didn't come right away, mind you, but he did a couple of days later, and it made all the difference—ended the shootout and decided the war.

Like I said, Dudley wasn't no Murphy-Dolan man; he'd had a bellyful of Jimmy Dolan and his bullies up to the hog ranches. What he was, though, was a Santa Fe Ring man, and by the time of the big shootout he knew Tom Catron had completely taken personal control of the Firm's operations, and Jimmy Dolan become just another feller around there—exactly what Winn Rigney told me was bound to happen. So there was Dudley over to the fort, just itching to get into the scrap and save Tom Catron's bacon, only there was some kind of law against such activity, unless it could be proved that everthing had broke down so completely that not even babies and their mothers was safe. Peppin had already asked him to come on, but Dudley sent back no by the black trooper. He said the same to Mrs. McSween, who had gone out to the fort to beg him. But O'Folliard's shot at his messenger made Dudley mad as a hornets' nest, and so he sent some white soldiers to find out who had fired it, and goddamn if we didn't fire on them as well. Wasn't from the house but somewheres up on the slopes. Well, that took it for the colonel, and next thing we knew town was just flooded with soldiers, and right opposite McSween's house was a twelve-pound howitzer pointing straight at it and Dad Peppin standing there amongst the soldiers and hollering at McSween to come out and surrender or the whole place would be blown to bits and everbody in there with it.

By this time I had already told Erasmo Chavez I wanted to change my position, that I judged I might be more useful over in the storehouse where the shooting angles on the Wortley might be better, and he said, bueno. Truth was that I wanted out of the house on account of I didn't want to be around them women and children when things got hotter, as all knew they was bound to. I had got accustomed to seeing men get hit by bullets and had some personal experience with that sort of thing, but this here was a different deal, and so when Chavez said bueno I straightaway went to the back of the house, gathered up my nerve, and then made a run for it. Wasn't but a few feet across, and then I dove behind the wall of the stable, which was attached to the storehouse. Nobody fired at me, and maybe by that point everbody's mind was tending to drift a bit, away from the murdering business we was there to do. So, that's where I was when the soldiers and their heavy guns come rolling in and Peppin begun hollering at McSween to come out and surrender.

There was two Mex boys that was already in there, kneeling on top of feed sacks that was stacked pretty near to the roof and looking through some slits made for ventilation. When I got up there with them, we seen McSween come just *flying* out, didn't have no hat on nor coat and was like a crazy man, all red and goggley-eyed and waving a sheet of paper, which he claimed was an order from the president himself that said no military man could get mixed up in civilian business unless the president said to. Peppin was heavy-armed and standing surrounded by soldiers while he listened to all this and had his hand on the breech of the cannon, threatening-like. To hit him you would have to get your bullet through a narrer space between soldiers, and I looked and looked, giving that a thought but concluded not to try. Glad I didn't now. But back then, in the heat of everthing and that hard bastard out there with his hand on the cannon and threatening to use it and blow my friends and the sisters and kiddies sky-high?

Hellfire, war'll make a man try for something that, later on, when that particular condition is long past, he'll think, 'Christ-a-mighty! I must have been *loco* to think that way.' And that's just what he had been, too, back then, when he was in battle and guns was popping all around him. You ever seen a cow that has got into a patch of locoweed? Some of 'em won't touch it—I don't know if it's the smell or what—, but one that eats it is snorting and sunfishing and crow-hopping like Midnight the Outlaw Horse out of chute eight in the rodeo. War is like locoweed to a man that's in the midst of it, and if he's lucky enough to live through it, he might have the occasion to think back on what he done—or didn't do, which was me: I didn't try for Dad Peppin and, like I say, I was glad later, especially one time when I was in Lincoln with my daughter, not that many years back, and we chanced across a couple with their little girl, at a fair or some such. Name was Wilson, and the little girl was Belle. Cute as a button she was and kept looking at my finger as kids will do. And so finally, I told her a elf had stole it from me one night, on account of I had lied to my folks. Turned out she was Dad Peppin's granddaughter, and I didn't mind lying to *her* long as I knew the truth, which was that I hadn't tried to dust her grandpa, though he might have deserved it. Probably did.

*

While all this was going on out front, me and the two Mex boys was big-eyeing the whole condition through the slits. I could savvy most of the shouting words but couldn't hear everthing, but then, you didn't have to: there was Peppin, surrounded by soldiers and with his hand on a cannon; and there was our man, all by himself, loco-looking and waving a slip of paper at Peppin. You didn't have to speak any American to see how this was going, and how it would turn out, and the two Mexes commenced jabbering, high and excited, and while they was, here come a pounding at the door, and we all quick swung our guns around that way. I thought it had to be our men; if it wasn't, we was done. And sure enough, a voice called one of them Mex boys by name and followed that up with some more remarks. Them boys come down off them sacks like bighorns off a mountain and flang up the bar. I stayed up top with my rifle ready, thinking that if it happened to be a trick, I was bound to take an enemy with me, if I could manage. But when the door went wide, I seen a bunch of Mexes, many of them over from the house, and in amongst them Hendry Brown. I was glad to spot him. Everbody but Hendry was waving their arms and shouting, and my two amigos rushed out to join them while Hendry was shouldering on through.

'They're leaving,' he hollers above all the commotion. 'All of them!'

And, by Godfrey, I seen straightaway he was right: all our Mexicans was running down towards the Bonito, and that couldn't be for no other reason than to run along it to where their horses was picketed beyond the Ellis store. I can't tell you now what I said to Hendry. Might have been, 'Greaser cowards' or the like. But looking back over your shoulder, so to say, you sometimes see the same thing different than when it was right in front of you—or you can, if you're built that way. If you're not, you're like to be stuck with all your old mistakes. So, what I would say now is, you could hardly blame 'em. After all, it's one thing to foller the Kid into a fight against them that has been making life mighty miserable for you and your kind, but it's another when it turns out your enemies has got the goddamn army lined up against you, and you're looking down the muzzle of a cannon. Takes a special sort of hombre to stand up to such a condition: got to be a hero or a fool, and most of us ain't really one or the other but somewheres in between. And remember, some of these boys that now was running didn't have reliable weapons, nor ones that shot the kind of ammunition we was getting from Tunstall's store.

Well, sir, that left me and Hendry just looking at their backs disappearing into the river cover and the door hanging wide with its bar down. We was figuring we was gone gooses, but then Hendry slams shut the door and drops the bar. 'Let's make them pay top dollar for it, pardner,' he says and commenced climbing back up the piles of crates and sacks. I done the same. And what we seen when we got up there was a shocker: for there was Dudley, giving orders to the soldiers, and then the guns was being wheeled about and the whole outfit slowly going eastward through town to what turned out to be a campsite opposite Ike Stockton's saloon, Peppin along with them. Half an hour later, and the road in front of the house was empty. But soon enough, we could hear shouts and sounds beginning to come from the upper end of town, and we scrambled around the sacks to look out that way and seen the enemy, running here and there. They'd seen what had happened with our Mexicans and then the soldiers going into camp, and they was now closing in for the kill. Two of them was breaking cover from down by the river, running towards the storehouse and stable, and me and Hendry fired on them but missed. One lost his nerve and run back to the cover, but the other kept on coming, trying to line himself up behind a shitter that was back there. Before we could get a good bead on him he got around the shitter and inside it, and I kept in firing, shooting blind, so to speak. Then we heard him holler.

'I got the son of a bitch!' I yelled to Hendry. 'Let's shoot that shitter till it falls to pieces and him with it!' Which is what we begun to do. That was the man I mentioned when I said I had shot a man in the war. What I didn't know then but later learned was that after I had wounded him in the hip, inside there, he drug himself to the hole and dropped down through it into the goddamn pit where our shots couldn't reach him, and that's where he stayed—poor bastard—until many hours thereafter when somebody heard him calling and helped him out of that Christ-awful condition. Makes a feller wonder what he wouldn't do to save his skin, don't it?

*

We was still shooting that shitter to splinters when we smelled the smoke. While Peppin and McSween was taking up everybody's attention the enemy had slipped around behind the house and poured wood shavings and coal oil on it and set a match to it. Some

76

said Jimmy Dolan done it, and it would have been like him, but whoever it was, it didn't take at first. So then, while the soldiers was getting turned around to go into camp, old man Boyle—as true a son of a bitch as ever stood in shoe leather—, he had got back there again, and this time she took, not roaring along but burning along steady towards that ell. The boys inside tried what they could to douse it, but now with our Mexes gone, they was surrounded, and it was impossible for them to throw any water out a window or a door without making themselves a target, and anyway there wasn't that much water left to throw. Hendry and me didn't know exactly what the situation was, but we did savvy that we was in a big wood building filled with sacks of dried grain, and if there was fire anywhere around, we was like to be blown sky-high.

What was to be done? If we was to run back to the house, what was we running toward? Likely we would be hit by crossfire. Or, we could stay put and be exploded or fried up. So, for what seemed a long time we didn't do nothing, just climbed down off them sacks and stood there, watching the smoke slide in through them slits and lie along the rafters like a big old snake. There was another door, a double one, on the river side of the building, but it was mostly blocked by a goodly set of barrels, and so we hadn't even give it a second thought. But now, with the smoke thickening up and the warmth along with it, we begun eyeing it. But here again, if we was to go out that way, we was going to run right down the muzzles of the enemy guns, which was surely positioned down in the river cover by now.

What we concluded to do was try clearing them barrels, so to give us at least a sliver of a chance to run out that way, the idea of being trapped like rats in the building not being a very appealing way to go. Hendry got up on the sacks on one side of the doors and me on the other, and we commenced rocking the barrels back and forth. Turned out they was empty, but being oaken, still was heavy. Well, we got them going quick enough—a desperate man has some strength he don't know he's got—, and once one tumbled, it caught the rim of another, and shortly we had a way cleared, if we wanted to use it.

Just then there come a terrific explosion from the house that shook the storehouse so bad it blew out a board of the roof, and it hung down, inviting yet more smoke in. Later, we learned that what had happened was a powder keg in the McSween courtyard had been touched off by the fire. Hendry looked at me and hollers over the fire and the gunshots, '*That's it!* This place is next! You foller me, George, and I'll clear us a way with this!' and he slaps that Yeller Boy he had.

Old Hendry. Somewheres around here I got a photograph of old Hendry, who likely saved my life with his nerve and that Yeller Boy he knew how to use to good effect. You wouldn't think it to look at him: clean of face and mild eyes. But he was just one of them men was never comfortable without there wasn't a gun involved someway—potting buffalo or another man who stood in the way of him. After the war here was done he went back north where he come from and fetched up in Medicine Lodge where he become marshal, and you would think that would be the right fit for him: had a gun and was ready to use it when trouble come to town. Wasn't enough. One day, him and a couple of others robbed the bank and killed the teller and the bank president. The town posse got after him right away, and after quite a chase they caught up with the robbers, and hung Hendry on the spot. But when he says to me to foller him, I was glad to do it—good man to foller. He flang open them doors and come out blazing, and I was right behind, firing a shot or two, though I hadn't any special target in view.

*

Used to be I would think back all the time on what happened next, both what I seen and what I later heard from Yginio Salazar, the only other feller left who went through it all. From the minute Hendry and me bust through them doors, on through that night that seemed like it would never end and there wouldn't be another sunrise on this old world—that was hell on earth, pardner. And like Blazer's Mill, I can recollect ever bit of it.

Mostly, it would come to me at night when I'd blow out the lamp and lie down in the darkness: them hellish things would come at me then like they was just happening. But not only at night. Other times I'd be out working by myself in the field, and find I'd been standing there so long the light had changed—just going through it like Job having to go through his tribulations over again. No more, though: I have come through to a place where I can talk about it if I choose, and not otherwise, but this was a long time coming to me. I don't know which of us is gladder, me or Cella, who had to bear a good deal when I would be thinking back and back.

I wonder how many others that went through it packed it around with them like me and tend to think not that many, judging from the way some behaved afterwards, and that includes men on both sides, like Jimmy Dolan and Jesse Evans on that side, and the Kid and Hendry on ours. I know Frank carried it some, because once or twice I asked him about it, but it was clear he wasn't eager to go back over it. Now me and Salazar is the only ones left, and I know he carries it, all right, along with a couple of slugs he got running out of McSween's burning house.

Anyways, what would always come back to me, first in them long after years, when I'd be lying there, sweating in the bed in the dark, or out in the field, was the look of Hendry's back, humping along in front of me in a red-checked shirt and a-pumping that Yeller Boy this way and that. In front of us, them bushes was just alive with flashes like they was full of lightning bugs. I could hear bullets whanging past me as we went, and I shot back once, just in the general direction of a flash. And how we made it into the cover is maybe the mainest thing that would cause me to toss and sweat in my bed and sometimes see dawn cracking. How *could* they have missed *both* of us? True, the light was getting bad as we run out, and there was the heavy smoke from the house. And then, Hendry was giving them something to consider with that Yeller Boy. But still . . .

Yet they did somehow miss us, and I went crashing down into that cover with the bullets ripping past overhead, but I couldn't keep my feet and quick went flying. When I landed I lost my hold on my rifle, but jumped up right away, and plowed ahead while trying to get my sidearm out. Wasn't no use in going back and hunting for the rifle, for I could hear shouting and crashing behind me and knew what that meant. The other thing I lost was Hendry and his Yeller Boy. I didn't hear nothing that would tell me he'd gotten hit, but I felt a terrible kind of lonesomeness, thrashing around in them bushes with all the enemy up above and knowing now that whatever become of Hendry, I was on my own.

I knew that somewhere down there was a little plank bridge over the Bonito, but since I didn't have no idea where I was, what with the house afire, the smoke, and dusk coming on, I calculated not to try to find it, but when I got to the river just jumped in feet first. River was still running pretty stiff for that time of year, and when I come up, it took me off my feet and down again I went. When I come up, I wasn't certain which was the right way and just started wading. Quick enough, though, I seen the fire up above me, so I turned about and got across to the far bank and crawled up like some hunted critter, which I sure-God was. My boots was so full of water I sat down to tug them off, and while I was at that I heard something to my right and stopped quick. Somebody was off there in the bushes, and he had heard me, too, because I could hear him trying to clear his gun. Looking that way, everything was a mushy sort of purplish-black, and

I couldn't see no movement. Then I couldn't hear nothing of the other man over that hellish commotion from up above, but knew he had to be near me—hell of a fix: there I was, had lost my rifle, didn't know if my sidearm would work, and didn't even have my boots on.

I don't know how long this condition continued—time drags when ever second seems like it could be your last. One thing was clear, though, which was that if I couldn't hear the other man down there, he couldn't hear me neither. But then, I thought I couldn't just sit here all night; the man nearby or them above would search for me sooner or later. I had to do something and so, desperate-like, I called out, low, somewhere between a call and a whisper, and even in that condition I knew I had to do better than that, so I tried again. 'Hendry! Hendry, that you? Don't shoot. It's me, George.'

Then there come back a voice, and I could tell it was Hendry, all right. 'What's the name of the horse I come over here on?' he says.

Well, *shit!* At that moment I thought I would be doing good to recollect my own goddamn name. 'Hell, I don't know, Hendry!' I called back, 'but I can tell you I rode old Dun over from San Patricio. You remember him, right?—stocky feller I traded for a while back?'

He tells me to stand up slow and with my hands high, and so I holstered my sidearm and done like he said. Then Hendry got up too with that Yeller Boy leveled, and we walked through the brush towards each other. 'Let's get out of here,' he says, and we made our way out of the brush and across a bit of pasture, running hard for the hills.

*

That night up on the bluffs was a terrible long one, as I said, made to seem longer on account of we never slept. There was a narrow ridge we got to after a climb, and I told Hendry I didn't care to go no further, even if we was maybe exposed where we had got to. I was that done in. There was some fair-sized rocks there we could crouch behind and look across to the town, which was lit up orange and yeller, and if you watched steady, you could see movement and could hear the shouts and shots and something else we couldn't put a name to, some kind of howl or wail that wasn't human, but more like what a coyote will make where it sounds like a baby crying. That and a lot of whooping. The wailing wasn't there all the time, just now and again, and when it come, Hendry would cup an ear, then shake his head. I don't know how it took him, but, me, when it come again it was like someone was sticking a knife in between my ribs—just *sharp*. And it went on all through the night, keeping company with the whoops and shots, until dawn commenced and then sunup, which seemed to take forever. By that point the whooping had pretty much quit and the shooting too, only a shot once in a while, like somebody found a slug left in his chamber and decided he might as well get rid of it. Then it was pretty much quiet up where we was, and we could peek around them rocks and see what was left.

Wasn't nothing left of the storehouse and only a part of the west wall of McSween's house. Rest was all gray and black ashes, still smoking, and here and there little spurts of flames. The store was yet standing, and there was some teams and wagons in front of it and men going in and out. Later on, we learned these was the enemy that was carrying off everthing valuable from the shelves and smashing up the rest.

So that was it, the end of the shootout, and there was mighty little left at our end of town whereas up to the upper end things looked pretty much as they had, with a crowd of men and horses in the road between the Wortley and the Firm's store. The trees along the Bonito was blocking much of our view down where the soldiers was camped, but we could see their horses and the little tails of smoke from their cook fires. Thirst was practically killing me, felt like, and I could see the Bonito sparkling along through the bushes but knew it would mean my life if I was to try to get down there for a drink. I don't know if I could have made it anyway, I was that stiff and sore. Ever muscle and bone in me screamed when I tried to shift position, and I begun to figure I had been hit somewheres. But trying to look myself over, I couldn't come across no blood anywheres, so asked Hendry would he look around my back and legs, which he done and shook his head. 'You look like an old cow-flop,' he says, 'but you ain't shot.'

Well, we knew we had to sit tight where we was and wait until another dark come: too many enemies still prowling about to chance moving anywhere. And so that's what we done on the longest day I ever lived—which followed the longest night: no water, no shade, not even a goddamn bush we might have put our heads near to get out of that terrible sun. Both of us had watches but both had stopped on account of the river (I still got mine, and so all these years after I know just when I jumped into the Bonito—eight-thirty-eight.), but damned if it didn't seem to us the day had stopped keeping time, just like them watches, with the sun just stuck in the sky where it stood, on top of us for hours. If our enemies had wanted to torture us, they couldn't have done better, for there we was, aching, thirsting, hungry, and our clothes stiff and heavy on us with dried mud, so it was like we was wearing metal shirts and pants like you see in them pictures of the knights of the olden time. At least, though, we had each other for company, and that was some comfort, though it's true we didn't do much socializing: it hurt even to talk. I do believe that if it hadn't been for Hendry I would have gone plumb crazy and run downhill to get to the river, hollering like an Indian, in which case I wouldn't be here telling you all this. As it was, that was as near as I ever want to come to being loco.

Everthing seemed evil, hurtful, wrong, black. I couldn't turn my mind to no place that had any comfort to it. Me and Frank had no doubt lost our spreads, and if the enemy hadn't found our mowing machine by now, they shortly would, along with all our stock and equipment. And now, they had also won the battle and the war, and we was doomed to be hunted men—no horses, but lightly armed, no supply of ammunition, no fighting friends, not even any hats. The enemy would ride us down like rabid curs, just like the Kid had predicted back at San Patricio.

Once in a while I'd take a peek around the rocks across to the town where it looked to me like the devil himself was mighty busy, carrying things here and there. Finally, in the afternoon there come some shouts and clanking noises, and looking in that direction, we seen the soldiers moving out of camp towards the fort, having done their duty here—by Dudley's lights, anyway. We watched that yeller dust from them rising up slow into the hot sky, and then finally they disappeared over the hills.

I turned to Hendry and said, 'Hendry, how in the name of Christ did we end up so?' He kind of cracked a little crook of a grin and shook his head. 'Luck,' he says. 'We didn't have it. I always figured the Kid to have it, but I guess this was one time he didn't. That's all she takes.'

*

When we judged it was safe to move, it was past sundown, and it took everthing I had not to just plunge on towards the Bonito, but somehow I held back, and we worked along slow till we got to the end of that ridge, then commenced angling down towards the river and that bit of pasture, which we run across, all bunched up. Hendry was in front, just like he had been when we busted out of that storehouse a million years ago, and I was trying to keep close, feeling like a hobbled horse. Where we reached the river was just short of the Ellis store, though still west of where we had picketed our horses the night before the shooting begun. We thought about moving on towards them to see if ours might still be there but concluded the enemy might be guarding them. But maybe just as important—to me, anyways—was the Bonito: I was mad to get at it, and when we got there we just waded in, waist-high, and begun scooping up handfuls to drink, coughing and choking on account of our throats was so dry. Finally, we climbed up the other bank to behind the store, not knowing who might be in it nor wanting to be taken as the enemy, whoever the enemy would look like to them inside. While we was coming across the yard careful, whenever there was a gust of breeze it brung to us this awful smell, sickly and heavy, something gone past ripe and into rot. Hendry turns to me and bares his teeth, disgusted. 'Death,' he says, and when he named it I knew he had it right and thought maybe it was a horse or mule that had been hit by a stray bullet. Whatever it was, we made our way through it and up to the back door of the store without being shot at, and I rapped quick while Hendry covered us. Nothing stirred inside, and all the shutters was pulled closed. I tried again, and the door cracked a sliver and whoever was there screamed and almost caught my nose in slamming the door to. It was Aunt Nancy Ellis. Then we heard Ike Ellis. 'Get away from that door,' he says, 'and I mean *now!*' We heard the hammer cocked, and we quick stepped aside, saying don't shoot, that it was Hendry Brown and George Coe. Then the door was flang open, and there was Ike with a shotgun leveled and Aunt Nancy behind him with her apron pulled up over her face and only her eyes showing, which was as big as saucers. Ike's was big, too, but he kept that gun level, then reached and grabbed my shirtfront and snatched me inside, Hendry coming right along behind and slamming the door to. Aunt Nancy began backing away from us with that apron held up and crying now behind it.

'By God, it's you, Coe!' Ike says. 'You ain't a ghost, I guess.' He looks at Hendry and lowers his gun and says, 'You boys has got to get out of here, pronto! They've killed almost everbody, and if they find you here, they'll kill you and us, too!' He didn't pull that gun up again, but I was afraid he was going to, so I put in quick that all we wanted was a bit of food, whatever was handy, and that we meant no harm. But he cut me off, said he was bound to protect Nancy and couldn't spare nothing. Then he says, 'What in hell has happened to you boys?' sort of gesturing to us. We couldn't catch his meaning, but then Aunt Nancy kind of comes to her senses and goes into another room and comes back with a scrap of mirror and hands it to me. When I looked into it I seen what made her scream so. I had been looking at Hendry for hours without noticing anything except a big long gash down his cheek where a branch or something had cut it, but when I got a look at my own face, why, it was something to behold: all black and streaked from caked dirt and sun and covered with scratches and cuts that was crusted over. No wonder Aunt Nancy had taken on so and Ike had thought we must be ghosts. And if he was right and all the rest of us had been killed, we might be ghosts, in a way of thinking. Of course, I wanted to hear about Frank, but Ike wouldn't stand for it and begun pushing us out the door. I wanted just a word, but Hendry grabbed my arm and turned me about just as Aunt Nancy come out of the kitchen with something wrapped in paper. 'Here,' she says and kind of throwed it at me, then scuttled away. It was a small block of cheese.

*

I believe I mentioned Yginio Salazar a while back. Well, like I said, him and me are the only survivors of the big shootout still alive. He's some years younger than me, and we're both still farming. He has a small place up a canyon west of Lincoln. Road to it goes right past Dad Peppin's place which now is run by the granddaughter, Belle Wilson. Salazar's a fine man. I used to visit him some a while back, though not much in recent years. One time Doc Blazer and me went out to see him. Doc wanted to get his story of how the shootout ended, on account of him and his wife was putting together a book on the war, and Salazar was the only one knew that part of the story. Rest of them was dead, like Old Man Boyle and Jimmy Dolan, who died a drunk. Or else they disappeared, like Kip Brown and Jesse Evans and Jim French. Mrs. McSween and her sister and the kids didn't see the end; they escaped before that. But one of those kids might not have escaped after all: he hung himself from a well curb up to Valentine, Nebraska, not that many years back, so maybe he couldn't stand thinking about it through the years, I don't know.

I had heard Yginio's story several times before Doc Blazer and me went up there, but I never asked questions. Didn't seem polite, somehow. But Doc asked him plenty and wrote down what he said. Also, Doc spoke some Mexican and could ask Salazar questions that way if something or other wasn't clear.

One thing that was clear from his telling was that after our Mexicans run off from the soldiers and the cannon, the Kid took charge of them that was left in the house. There was another four or five of us that had been up in the Torreon—that included Frank—, but they was cut off from the house by the enemy and ended up hiding in the loft of a barn behind Juan Patron's, and during the night Hendry and me spent up on the ridge they slipped over the mountains and made it safe back to San Patricio. Them left in the house with the Kid was a man name of Morris worked for McSween; Tom O'Folliard—only death could pry him away from the Kid; a relative of Chavez's; Jim French; Salazar and one or two other Mexes; and McSween, who was useless, if he wasn't worse. After the women and children left, the Kid corralled everbody in the kitchen and said all wasn't lost, that they could still maybe escape. So, there you have him, steady as ever, like I said. His plan was to have two groups run out of the house in different directions, first one, then the other. The first bunch was him, O'Folliard, and some others, and the second included McSween and Salazar. While he was saying all this, McSween just sat in the corner with his head in his hands, staring at the floor. When the Kid asked him was he game to try, McSween looked up but didn't say nothing, so the Kid went right on, and him but a boy, remember—maybe nineteen if he was that.

Then he went to McSween and got him on his feet, and shortly after that he and his bunch run out, firing into the night. McSween went to the door, but then he didn't go no further, just stood there looking out, and couldn't nobody get past him. So, they missed their chance, and when somebody finally pushed McSween out, the enemy was waiting. He was hit five or six times and killed before he hit the ground. Morris got shot in the head and killed. One of the Mexes was bad wounded but not killed until after it was all over and the enemy was going around, kicking corpses to make sure all was dead; they seen him breathing yet and shot him dead. Salazar was hit four times. One shot went all the way through his side. One hit him in the arm and another in his shoulder. I forget where he said the other was, but when he went down it was almost on top of McSween.

When he come to he was looking at a pair of boots which it turned out was Andy Boyle's who was busy kicking McSween's corpse around while he hollered hoorah and drank out of a bottle. Salazar quick shut his eyes to play dead, and good thing, too, because Boyle stepped over to give him a boot in the ribs. How that boy kept from screaming is a wonder, but Boyle's devilment probably saved Salazar, on account of he passed out again and so looked really dead. He must have been out quite a while, because when he opened his eyes again it was getting gray, and he quick shut his eyes again on account of there was boots again near his face. So, he just lay there in terrible pain, listening to the boots scuffling the dirt and—can you believe it?—*fiddle music!* Them bloodthirsty fuckers had two black fiddlers playing "Turkey in the Straw," or some such, while they passed bottles of Taos lightning amongst them and once in a while give a corpse another good boot. *That* was the wailing sound we had heard off on the ridge but couldn't place: fiddle music! Through all that killing they had them two black bastards playing so they could dance and drink and celebrate wiping out our side. Of all the terrible things that commenced with the treatment of Tunstall's corpse, this here somehow seems almost the darkest one.

Next thing he hears is two men nearest him about to get into a fight over something, and while he's laying there it becomes clear they was arguing about McSween. One feller says it wasn't decent to let chickens peck out his eyes, while the other was saying the bastard had it coming and then some. The first one shoved the other who fell over Salazar, and when he rolled off, Salazar took a peek and seen the other man shooing the chickens away. He was a fat, burly feller, Salazar said, and when he pictured him for Doc Blazer and me, I knew right off it had to be Kip Brown. Well, it wasn't a time for me to say nothing about Brown and that I knew him for the shit he was, but afterwards, when I was by myself, I had a good think about that. And what come to me was considerable upsetting, because all these years I had been having a good old time hating Kip Brown, and here it had been shown that he wasn't a *complete* shit but that somewhere, way down in his being, to put it that way, there was a bit of good stuff. And if that could be true of Kip Brown, who couldn't it be true of? I don't know yet about this, but I have to wonder whether all them years of hating Brown was necessary to bring me to a place where I can remember his treatment of me on the trail, but then go on to allow there was a bit of good mixed in with all that shit.

V

S alazar was able to crawl away while all them fuckers was drunked-up, and the fiddlers was still sawing away as the light begun to come on, just like nothing had even happened. But when he got across to the house of a relation it was a bit like when me and Hendry knocked on the door of the Ellis place: they looked out and seen this bloody *thing* clawing at the door, and they screamed—thought it was something out of the grave, as naturally they would. That house wouldn't let him in, but the one next to it would and saved his life.

Us, we wasn't crawling like poor Yginio, but was bad beat up, making it over the mountain and down to San Patricio well past sundown—running across open places, clambering, ducking into cover when we seen a horseman or a sheepherder. That is some condition to find yourself in where you don't know who is harmless and who is like to kill you. It's like that man in the Bible: ever man's hand turned against you, or so it seems. Just hellish. We made it, but before we was allowed to enter the village we was met by armed men, some with guns, others with big knives or pitchforks, but I picked out one I recognized from the shootout and spoke to him. He didn't speak American but anyway recognized me and run and brought back Jaramillo, the water chief, who held up a lantern and looked us over and then led us into the village, which was quite a different place from what we'd left days before. Houses was shut up and dark, same with the cantinas, and only men outside. Jaramillo spoke good

American and told us what we wanted to hear: that some of our friends was safe on the other side of the bridge. When we got over there we found the Kid, O'Folliard, Jim French, and Charlie Bowdre, but I was naturally looking and looking for Frank. Then I seen him, kind of taking form out of the gloom, which put me in mind again of ghosts, of me and Hendry at the Ellises'. But he was real enough and come towards me with a smile, and we struck hands real firm and stayed that way a long moment. Frank was never what you'd call a real outgoing sort, but I couldn't miss that he was just as glad to see me as I was him. At that moment it felt an awful long ways for us to have come from that bed we shared back in Queen City when we was boys, staring up through lamplight at that fox he'd shot.

There wasn't no room in the casita we'd bunked in before. The Kid was already in there with Jim French and O'Folliard. We couldn't go down along the river with Charlie, on account of he was staying with Manuela's people. Frank was bunking out back in the orchard, and Jaramillo got me and Hendry some blankets, and what with them and the high grass of summer it felt like heaven to us after the last days when we had never so much as looked at a sure-enough bed nor a blanket.

I don't recollect another thing till well past the next noon when voices woke me, and I rolled over and looked around to find the Kid and Hendry and Jim French sitting next to the tree I was lying under, smoking and drinking coffee. I laid there, trying to make sense of the whole picture—where I was, where I'd been, what we was doing here, and where 'here' was. And the longer I looked, the worse we all seemed. Jim French always looked like he'd been rode hard, so there was nothing new there. But staring foggy-eyed at the Kid, I had never seen him looking so seedy. One side of his face was all burned and blistered and infected with boils, hair was sticking out like twigs from a crow's nest, clothing all raggedy and mud-caked. The only thing about him that looked regular was the walnut butt of that Thunderer he had tucked in his waistband. Rest of him looked like some tramp that hadn't seen water in quite a spell. He was smoking steady between sips of coffee and picking at his teeth with a pared matchstick. And while I was swimming upwards towards all this, like I'd been down in a well, I thought, 'By Godfrey, we have sure enough hit bottom.' Then Frank come out of the casita, seen me awake, and turned back to get me a cup of coffee, which sharpened me up a bit. The rest of that day I spent hunting ways to put myself back together, taking a bath in the river, and washing my clothes while I was at it. The Kid asked me what I needed, and I said some saddle soap for my boots, gun-cleaning equipment, and just about anything I could get to eat. Funny thing was that while I did need them things, the thing I most wanted was something I didn't think I could ask for, and that was just a clean pair of socks. Doesn't seem like anything truly needful, but there are times where something real common-like is all you really want. Anyway, the Kid said if I could sit tight a while, he would have some of my needs seen to, which they was. But it turned out to be a good two weeks before I had a horse, a hat that fit, a rifle that worked proper, and even then I wasn't near put back together, but then none of us was, excepting the Kid.

He had got what the Mexicans call a *curandera*, who come to him and worked on his face, popped them boils, worked lotion into it, and it seemed like overnight he looked more like himself. He got his hair trimmed and his clothes washed and patched where needed. The last thing was that big roan of his, which Erasmo Chavez brung across the bridge on a lead rope one morning. The Kid come out of the casita like he had been expecting this, and that horse went right up to him and laid its forehead on the Kid's chest. It was a sight to see, and I said so to Frank, who kind of grunted that it was all fine for the Kid, but what about the rest of us? They right away brung the Kid a saddle and a hackamore, and he swung up on the roan and galloped across the bridge and on out of the village and was gone so long we begun to wonder if he had gone back to Lincoln to finish the fight against our enemies.

But, no, he'd only been away on business, so to say, and after a few days here he come again to tell us he was here to collect a few things and then was bound for the Seven Rivers area to gather some horses and drive them to Las Cruces for sale. When he was finished with that, he said, we was all due for a real *baile* down to the old Chisum headquarters at Bosque Grande: it was time for our side to get together, have ourselves a high old time, and then get back on the trail of the enemy. So, if Peppin and them thought they had seen the last of the Regulators, they was damn fools, that we had only changed our name to the 'Ironclads.' 'We never quit,' the Kid said, 'and they can't break us up, on account of our loyalty is like iron.' He went on like that while he was tying up some things on the roan, kind of speaking to us over his shoulder most of the time. Then he mounts up and turns the roan about real sharp. 'See you boys down at the old Bosque in three, four days,' he says, and then off he goes again, over the bridge and out of the village, sitting that roan pretty as ever.

Well, all this quick news didn't sit so well with some. Charlie and Manuela was one. Manuela was there with all her family, including Nazarina, and as soon as the Kid had gone, she lit into Charlie good. Like I say, she was a fiery gal and had been after Charlie for quite some while to quit all this fighting and settle down in the village. I didn't get most of what she said, it being both Spanish and American, but it sounded like what a Gatling gun might have if it was spitting out words instead of slugs. Hendry and Dash Waite took the news somber-like, shaking their heads and Dash muttering that he didn't know about going on with the fighting, especially now with the army into it on the other side.

'I got one horse that can go some,' he says, pointing at the corral through the trees. 'I got a half-day horse that can go that long when the good horse can't. I got two sidearms; one is dependable, and the other one I took off a dead man, and it ain't. So, I don't know as I'm truly set up to be one of these Ironmen he's talking about collecting over to the Bosque—and that ain't even figuring in the cannon.'

'Course, Tom O'Folliard was all for the Kid's new plan, which he made plain with his usual 'fucks' and 'shits,' but then, you would have to figure on that. Others was talking back and forth, about who was in and who wasn't sure, and then we all broke up. Charlie and Manuela's family with Nazarina was going back along the river towards their houses. I had seen her several times before this but always at a distance, and she had always signed me off with a flick of her hand, but yet I was hoping to get off with her again some night soon. Frank caught me looking after her as she went and spoke sharp to me about it, saying we had important business to discuss, about what we was going to do now. So then him and me moved off through the orchard towards the hills, and when he judged we had gone far enough he stopped and faced back towards the village, and I begun to do the same. '*No*,' he says, stern. 'You watch that way,' pointing towards the hills. When he started talking, it was so low I had to lean towards him to get what he was saying.

'Dash has got it right,' he whispered. 'This here fighting is *shit*. Being shot at is shit. Being a wanted man is shit—we can't go nowhere! That's all fine for the Kid—I don't believe he knows to do otherwise. O'Folliard's a fool and is like to be dead any day now. Me, I want to live peaceable and raise my crops, goddamn it! We didn't come down here for this.'

Well, of course, I had to agree with him on everthing. All I had to do was to think back to that hellish night me and Hendry spent up on that ridge and the hellish day after that. This wasn't no kind of life, but it did seem more or less what the Kid had in mind for our bunch, running, dodging, hiding out, and meanwhile picking off the enemy, one at a time. But Frank said he had been giving all this considerable thought even before the Kid told us his plans. He had been scheming to find a time to slip back into Lincoln, leave our affairs with Uncle Ike Ellis, who was a dependable sort, and then to get on up to the Sugarite fast as we was able, to join up with Lou and Al Coe. Someday, he said, we might be able to come back here and work our land again after things had cooled down, but if that day never come, then maybe Uncle Ike could arrange to sell it for us, and we might get at least a few dollars out of the whole sorry mess. But while he was figuring a way to talk this over with Uncle Ike, he said he believed it might be real dangerous for us to let on to anybody in our bunch how we was thinking, and that we had best join the others down at the old Chisum place.

'You never know about the Kid,' he said when we had finished talking plans. 'You don't know how he's likely to take this. But I do know this much: I wouldn't want to find that for some reason or other he had come to regard me as his enemy.'

*

When Frank and me showed with the others at the Bosque, we seemed like members in good standing, you might say, of the Ironclads, but we had our secret plans set. We was still outlaws along with the rest, but we was fixing to become outlawed outlaws as soon as we judged it safe, splitting off from all our pardners and making dust for the Sugarite—quite a condition to be in. But, my, what a time at the old Bosque! Place wasn't near as handsome as what Chisum had set up at South Spring and maybe had been let go a bit since he'd turned it over to his brother Jim, who was a tough old bird but didn't think real big like John. Jim had told the Kid the place was his for a few days,

and then him and his wife found themselves someplace else
to be when our gang piled in: Doc and Dash, Jack, Jim French,
O'Folliard, Hendry—all that hard-hitting bunch together again.
Jugs of whiskey, two fire pits going day and night with beef
and sheep turning on spits. We had two fiddlers, playing for
their lives, and me and Frank took a turn on their instruments,
though we was both real rusty. There was a guitar player over
from Sumner, all the gals a sane feller could require, and not a
white one amongst them. When Frank and me got there things
was already running fast, and so we had a bit of a time wading
in, the music going furious and the boys swinging them gals
high, but we soon got our feet under us. The Kid was there in the
midst of it, and ever once in a while our eyes would kind of lock
a moment, and I would wonder could he see inside my head to
what I had in mind. I know that'll sound loco to you, but if you
had known him and seen them eyes, you might not have been
so sure yourself, neither.

Well, she finally ended after a few days, and maybe you've been
in that condition, where a big shindig closes up, and you take a
look around and everthing and everbody looks like shit, and you
know you do, too. Like as not, there'll be someone there to hand
you a jug and say, 'Let's have one more for the good times,' or
something like. Or it might be you that has that stupid thought.
But it don't work, of course—that last drink, I mean: the thing is
just done. Here the *baile* was done, all right, but looking around
me that morning I believed I seen others besides the Coe boys
that had come to know our old ways was ending here, that the
trails was forking away, whatever the Kid had in mind with the
Ironclads. When I seen that, maybe I had another drink from the
jug—might have. Trying to calm my nerves, you see. But while
we was hanging around, not doing much of anything, with the
gals mostly gone or else looking considerable played out and
the musicians, too, Dash Waite joined Frank and me and some

others that was sitting in the cool of the ramada on the north side of the main building, smoking and gabbing just a bit. Somehow, he looked a bit more spruce than the rest of us, hair pushed back under his hat and his shirt tucked in. He squats down amongst us, rolls a smoke, and somebody hands him a light. We sat that way a spell when Dash up and says that for him this was where one trail ended, and it was time for him to take another. He was going back to the Nations, he told us, where he'd come from and where he had plenty of family.

'My ass is tired,' he said, 'and I'm tired all over—tired of being shot at, tired of shooting back. Doc said the same, said he might soon go on up to Kansas City.'

'The Kid know this?' Jim French said. I could've kissed him, dirty, stubbly feller that he was, because that was *just* what I wanted to find out and Frank along with me. Dash nodded yes, said he'd spoken to him not many minutes ago. So then I wanted like anything to learn how the Kid had taken it but quickly concluded that if Dash was here and not laying out somewheres with holes in him, the Kid must have taken it okay. But what if Doc also had spoken to the Kid? Might be one thing for Dash to say he was quitting, another for Doc, but then here come Frank and me. You savvy my thinking here? Like Frank had said back in the orchard at San Patricio, you never knew about the Kid, and I had a flashing thought back to that night when me and Nazarina heard him, sliding through the grasses in his socks, and maybe hunting us with that Thunderer cocked.

Well, when he finished his smoke Dash up and left, going on to the Nations where, so I understand, he made a good name for himself—become an important man amongst his people. That left us, Hendry, Jim French, Tom Pickett, Jack Middleton, O'Folliard, and I forget who else—maybe Billy Wilson—hanging around the place, waiting on the Kid who had ridden out by himself, as he had lately a habit of doing, like he had got all he wanted of his pardners for a time and wanted to be solitary for a spell. There was some talk of riding up to Beaver Smith's, which was a saloon up to the old fort, but me and Frank said we wasn't up for that, and here Frank broke in and told the boys we was thinking of going up to the Sugarite where we had family. He said we missed farming and was tired of all this running around. Nothing definite—just a notion we had been thinking about. O'Folliard laughed and said he had got enough of following a mule's ass through the dirt when he was back in Texas, and that he'd rather get shot out of the fucking saddle than to try that kind of life again—about what you could expect from him, but I wonder whether there wasn't others that had about that same opinion, Hendry for one. I have often wondered whether that style of living—all the hard riding, hard drinking, fighting, hitting the hog ranches, and so forth—gets into a man like needing a drink all the time. You might get so you couldn't do without it, and the idea of having some neat little place fenced around and a garden with a wife and kiddies—all that would seem terrible boresome. It sure didn't seem so to me at that moment, though, for there I was, a hunted man who couldn't go near his own place and didn't even have all his fingers left. Compared to what I had become, even the sight of a mule's ass didn't seem so bad. Besides, I had Frank for company, and that was a steadying thing.

With Dash gone, Frank and me was a little betwixt and between, as they say, waiting with the others for the Kid to return but yet at the same time wanting to get away before he did, and so finally we got our things together, which didn't take long, having lost about everything we owned except three horses. When we swung up, O'Folliard hollered that we'd be back, and Frank says, maybe so, and that if the Sugarite didn't suit us, then the boys could look for us again.

That was it. We just hit the trail up towards Anton Chico, leaving all our pardners behind, them who had been through the whole mess with us. Might seem strange to you, sitting here with your automobile and roads that can take you just about anywheres and back again in no time. But back then, like I earlier remarked, folks just drifted in and out of your life like tumbleweed. And right now we're seeing that same thing with this awful dry spell we're in—folks drifting here and there about the country with everthing they own just strapped to some raggedy old truck. But I look for this to end; one of these old days we're bound to hit a spell of favorable weather, and folks will stay put, and send down roots.

*

After sundown we made Anton Chico where we had a friend name of Johnaston Banks we knew would take us in. He ran a stable, him and a Mexican woman, his wife having run off with one of the hands, leaving him with two kids. That Mex gal would make you stiff as a billygoat just looking at her, and while they wasn't married, she was a good cook and mothered them kids better than their natural mother ever had. Considering everthing, it looked like a good stopover for us: good chow, good beds, our horses seen to—and that Mex woman.

Next morning she was giving us coffee with goat's milk, which is tasty if you're used to it, when Banks comes in to tell us that the Kid was here in town and had won big last night at monte. Well, sir, there we was, and here *he* was, somewheres right around us. Anton Chico wasn't a big place, nor is it now, and there wasn't no sense thinking to slip out without the Kid noticing. As usual Frank didn't say much, but we was both full of thoughts of how it would have been best if things hadn't fallen as they had, with us ending up in the same place as the Kid—a small town in this great big country and us trying to make a getaway from him. As you can see, these was also probably foolish thoughts, useless. The only thing left for us to do was what we done: just saddle up and take the main street north out of town to where our trail forked east. So, we rode out on that cloudy morning, being cautious not to look like we was in much of a hurry, but my insides was in a real rumble and was curdling that goat's milk as we ambled along. Just when we had reached the last of the buildings and could about see ahead to where the trail fork lay, we was waylaid.

'Hello, boys.'

It was him, who had come out of somewheres behind us. We wheeled around on them words, which was said so soft it was almost like he was singing them, '*Hel-lo, boys* . . .' I can hear them just now. And there he was, standing on the porch of a café with a toothpick in his mouth and a smile on his face. Well, we wheeled about, all right, but that don't make us cowards, those being jumpy times in the territory, and I make no doubt that if we had come up on the Kid that way, he'd have whipped around himself—though the fool that had called to him would quick have been staring up hard at his long home. Me, I might have done something almost as foolish, such as claiming we had been hoping to run across him. Not Frank, though. There were numerous times them days when I was thankful for Frank with his older years, and back in the times I'm telling of, you mostly didn't get to have any older years if you didn't have some steadiness that had come to you along with them. I can't now recall a genuine foolish man out here that lived to be an older one. So here, all Frank says was, howdy, then tells the Kid we had stopped overnight here with a friend, and was on our way up to the Sugarite to visit family we hadn't seen since they was run off the Ruidoso by the Firm.

'Them bastards has fixed life for a good number,' the Kid says, 'but someday soon they'll get theirs.' Then he takes that toothpick out of his mouth and points it northward. 'In the meantime,' he says, 'I'll travel on with you a ways, if you'll wait till I get my horse.' We said we would and waited there in the road, making quite a big thing out of rolling some smokes. Finally, he come out of an alleyway on the roan, and I recollect that at that ticklish moment what struck me most was what a handsome stud the Kid was up on. Shows you what a curious thing a man's mind can be, when at a place where for some very important reason you ought to have yourself at a full attention, instead you might find that you're watching a bluebird settle into a juniper or a butterfly flittering over a field. But somehow we got through it and commenced slow-trotting out of town, me wondering just what the Kid had in mind in saying he would travel with us a ways. And what popped into my head just then was Morton and Baker that was traveling with the Kid into Blackwater Canyon, and never come out the other side. But the Kid wasn't lagging behind or acting funny; he was just riding along as you would at the beginning of a journey. And then we come to our east-running trail, where we reined in. I said we hoped to meet up again when we'd had a visit with our kinfolks, and Frank threw in that if we found we liked it well enough up there, we could get word to him through our friend Banks, and then he could come on himself and see how it suited him. The Kid smiled a bit, and it come to me for the first time that maybe the reason he never smiled real wide is on account of he felt funny about them rabbit teeth of his.

'No,' he said, 'I don't think that likely. You boys was farming when I come to know you, and I expect that's what you'll end up doing in that country or somewheres. It's what you know best. Me, this is what I know.' He sort of waved toward everthing you could see around you: the town, which wasn't much, the range, the blue mountains way off. And I think what he meant by that wave was all the cattle and horses that was out there for him to rustle, and the women and monte games in Anton Chico and Cimarron and Fort Sumner and San Patricio and Tascosa, and them other places he frequented. That's what he knew like we knew farming. I don't know what else he could have meant. But then, there was always more to him than any of us could figure.

That was the last we ever seen of him and I hope the last I ever will see of him, on account of he has no doubt been in Hell a long while now, and I do hope I don't end up riding with him again on that unending range.

VI

When we got up to the Sugarite, Lou and Al made us welcome, just as before. Things were now better up there, they told us. Ernest had died, and even before that happened the other cattlemen had eased off on the farmers on account of Clay Allison had taken it into his head to befriend the sodbusters up that way.

Allison, as you may have heard, was a ready killer. How he ended up in the Sugarite area I have no idea, nor did anyone seem to know just why he decided to throw in with the farmers. Maybe there wasn't no special reason, except this: Allison was a drunk. So here you have a man who is violent, who is a known killer, drifting through the country, killing a man here, a man there, then moving along like he has accomplished his mission by killing poor old Abner—or whoever—in Cimarron City, and so just moves along. You take a man of such a description, which I believe fits Allison, and then you fill him with forty-rod—what they called whiskey when I was a boy back in Missouri—and there's no telling what he's likely to do or who he's likely to befriend or get crosswise with. Here, he decided to take offense with Ernest, but instead of shooting him, he was said to have invited him to take coffee with him at the Red River Station. They sat there, both of them drinking cup after cup, and Allison told Ernest he understood the farmers believed they had rights to their spreads and that until it was proved otherwise he—Allison—was aiming to stick around and protect them. Ernest said that was jake with him, probably figuring it was best to play for time and wait for this killer to move along. But then Ernest died, and not long after that Allison died, too: he had been in Cimarron, drinking all day, then got into his wagon to drive back to wherever he was putting up. On the way, he fell out, and his team pulled a wheel over him and broke his goddamn neck. Fact. So, that's where matters stood when we got there, and nobody really could figure what might happen next, but Lou and Al put us right to work.

Harvest comes early in that north country, and there was plenty of work to go around, but everbody could see I didn't take to it as I had previous. The brothers seen it but didn't say nothing, probably thinking that shortly I would change my ways and be the George they had known. And Frank, he would see me, standing off by myself in the fields, looking away toward nowheres. Plainly, I was different—and I am *still* different—on account of what me and Hendry went through. I didn't know that then; I only knew I was goddamned uncomfortable anywhere I was. And the longer I stayed on, the worse it got, especially with the crops laid by and more time than ever hanging on me, though, if you have ever been on a ranch or a farm, then you know that if you have time on your hands, pardner, you ain't pulling your weight, as there is *always* something needs doing.

I just told you that Clay Allison was a drunk. Well, I was a good way started down that same trail myself come winter's end. Even back when Frank and me was helling around up to them hog ranches I wasn't a heavy daily drinker, though once started I could hold my own. Yet now I found myself drinking as much as I could at supper, till the jug was put up and then the next morning not feeling exactly like a top hand. Taken steady that way, whiskey will wear a man down, even a young one. Then, one day Lou comes to me and says he wants me to take the team and wagon into Cimarron for supplies. Well, it was clear by his list that they was needed all right, but I had been up there plenty long enough to know that when supplies was to be got, their hand Virgilio customarily seen to that: they was giving me time to be off by myself, and figuring that if I wasn't doing my share around the place, they could at least get some use out of me by sending me for needful things.

Next morning early I set off. It was raining, though not too hard as yet. Nothing new there: that early spring it seemed like ever day it did something—rain, sleet. . . . It was like God knew my troubles and was telling me He did, and who's to say He didn't? Just north of Cimarron it commenced coming down so hard it was like bullets on a west wind. Through it I made out a lone horseman and two packhorses behind. He had pulled up and had the horses half-turned, like he might have been considering going back to town and letting the storm blow itself out. Then he seen me and we signed slow and come on, him with his hat dropped over his ears with the heavy water, and as we did there begun to seem something about him that I knew from somewheres.

It was Hendry. We parleyed there in the saddle, hollering at each other through the weather, and I made up the rest of his mind for him, and we went back into town, put up at the hotel, and got a jug for the room. Then we talked on through the night about what we had been through, about my troubles up on the Sugarite, and what had brought him up to where our trails once again had crossed.

Right off I learned he was finished with the Regulators or whatever the Kid was calling them now, and so was most: Jack Middleton, who was bad crippled yet from Blazer's Mill; Dash, Doc, Jim French. That left Tom O'Folliard and a couple or three new fellers Hendry didn't take much stock in. There was one called Wilson and another went by Dirty Dave that Hendry said he had never seen near water. They planned to go on rustling stock, especially from Chisum, who the Kid said owed him money for the work he'd done against the Firm.

'I don't have a high regard for Chisum,' Hendry said, 'as I think he was always in it for himself and was just using Tunstall and McSween.' He said the Kid was just another pony on Chisum's string, and that Chisum had rode him about as far as was useful. 'It ain't healthy rustling from the Jingle-Bob,' he said. 'Chisum himself don't kill men that goes against him, but has plenty of others that will do that for him.' With the war over, he said the old enemies was getting together to split the difference. 'You watch, George,' he says, 'them big boys are fixing to carve up this whole country amongst themselves. Sides change, but that don't. The Ring and them will come out on top.'

We went on like that, talking over the big shootout and all. 'We pret' near got killed for nothing,' he says, pointing at my hand. 'You ain't even got all your fingers. Hell, I like riding hard, shooting, as well as the next man—took to it natural, seems like. But damn if I'm going to stop a bullet for my boss, and then come to find out he'd as soon shoot me himself, if he found he needed to. Hell with that.' He said there was plenty of boys in the Civil War that for a few dollars went and fought in another man's place and got killed and was buried any old spot where nobody could ever find them, so that it was like they had never lived at all. 'That ain't me,' he said, 'not any more, at least.'

The last straw for him was the killing of lawyer Chapman, who was working for Mrs. McSween, trying to get her justice against them that killed her husband. It was a thing so senseless it caused him to see he had to leave all that mess behind him and set out for new territory.

It had happened only a few weeks back on the main street in Lincoln, and the way he told it a bunch of fellers, enemies in the war, was having drinks together and swearing they would be like brothers ever afterwards: the Kid, Jesse Evans, Billy Matthews, Dolan, O'Folliard, and a man named Campbell. After a while they decided they'd had enough at whatever place they was drinking and went down the street to Juan Patron's for more. That's when they come across the lawyer feller. Hendry heard that this Chapman only had but one arm and was an excitable sort. And you know how it is when you're having a hell of a time with your friends, and you come across another feller who ain't quite so happy. You might try to jollify him some, but if he happens not to take to that, well then, pardner, it's surprising how quick things can turn ugly, which is what happened here with Chapman. Maybe it was Jesse Evans tried to get Chapman in the mood, yanking him this way and that, and when Chapman got angry, they all pulled out their sidearms and commenced shooting down near his feet so as to get him dancing. You can picture it, can't you?—bunch of drunked-up fellers crowding around a sober man and firing off pistols. A purely combustible condition, and that's just how it turned out. Somebody—Hendry didn't hear who— shot Chapman, and killed the poor fucker. The Kid told Hendry he didn't see who done it as he had dropped back and turned aside to light a smoke, and you'll remember the Kid was never a drinking sort, and so wouldn't have been one of them doing all the pushing and shoving and shooting. Whoever it was, he fired so close it caught Chapman's coat on fire, and down he went. And Jesse, who was ever a headstrong sort, pours whiskey on him, whether to put out the fire or make it bigger, who knows? (Jesse has to be long gone by now, but in his time he was some tough hombre, and the last anybody seen of him, he had broke and run from what they call a chain gang, down in Texas.)

Anyway, they all run off down the street to Juan Patron's, leaving poor Chapman there in the night, sending up flames out of himself. Hard to get any more senseless than that, but when you put it together with the killing of Tunstall, they're about the same sort of thing. And so, if Buck Morton's shot at Tunstall was the first one of the war, then this here was the last. And all for what? you might be asking yourself. You tell me: I been turning it all over in my mind for half of a century and would be glad to have an answer at last.

Some said it was Evans done it; sounds like it to me. Some said the Campbell feller. And some still are saying it was the Kid, though I don't think you'll find many of these folks coming from our side of things. It's true, the Kid was seen over the body after the others run off, like he was either looking for something or trying to put out the fire. Hendry believed the Kid when he said he never done it, and whatever your opinion of him, I don't think you would take him for a scavenger. A killer, sure enough, but no vulture.

Well, as you can imagine, that brought the new governor down from Santa Fe pronto: After all, Lew Wallace was supposed to have control of a territory where a lawyer on a peaceable mission wouldn't be shot down and set afire on the main street of a county seat. So, he gets down there quick, makes an assay, so to put it, and orders the arrests of the Kid, Evans, Campbell, and Matthews. Kimball, who was the new sheriff in place of Peppin, quick enough finds Evans and Campbell and jails them up to the fort, where they didn't stay long. That bastard Dudley had them under what you might call a light guard, and one fine morning the prisoners didn't make roll call. That was the end of that, a mystery that has never been solved and now won't ever be.

So what Wallace done then when he seen what a terrible tanglement things was in the county was to issue a proclamation that said that them who was in the war on any side was pardoned. Simplest thing he could have done, sort of sweeping all of it off to the side so folks could get on with their lives. But not quite all was pardoned. 'Not the Kid,' Hendry told me. 'Not Jack, not Charlie, not Doc, not Dash.' He took another jolt from the jug and says, 'And not me and not you and not Frank. We are all still wanted, on account of Blazer's Mill where Roberts was said to be carrying good paper with our names on it.' This was what brung him up to where our trails crossed: he was on his way out of the territory and advised me and Frank to do something similar.

By that time we had talked and drunk through the night, and the light in the window was like old iron. Rain was hard as ever, but there was Hendry, getting himself together to head northward, bound for Missouri where I believe he was from. I seen him to the door of the hotel but not across all that slop to the stable; we said our goodbyes on the porch. He was heading away from trouble, he told me again, and in a way he was, if by that you mean the trouble he already knew about. But there's some that seem to pack trouble along in their saddlebags, like an old sickness that become a part of them, and Hendry was one. Up there in Medicine Lodge, he unpacked that particular bag and ended up hanging. I ain't the man to judge him, but I am obliged to hope the Good Lord takes into account the grit and goodness I seen in him in them long hours of the big shootout. No man alive though can tell us just how them scales gets balanced out.

*

Me, I was still packing along my own troubles and was obliged to continue that till I could figure out a way to rid myself of them other than to get drunked-up enough to forget them for a few hours. So, after saying goodbye to Hendry, wasn't nothing for it but to do my errands in Cimarron and haul everthing back to the spread, which looked more dismal than before I left. And of course, right away I had to tell Frank that we was yet wanted men, and what did he think we ought to do? He said to let him think on that, and a couple of days later over supper he spoke to Lou and Al about it. They thought it unlikely the law would come up almost into Colorado hunting us, and Frank thought the same. They all agreed our best move was none at all, but to stay put, keep our heads down, and wait to see what developed down in Lincoln County with the new sheriff and the new governor.

Still, nobody was real happy to get Hendry's news, but I was more unhappy than any of them. Lou and Al was all involved in working their land, and from the first Frank had seemed to take to the new conditions and fit right in, whereas all I could do was mope about and think back on all the things I had left behind, where maybe what I should have been thinking was that I was still alive and had most of my fingers and toes. But I couldn't. Here I was, a wanted, hunted man whereas, to hear Hendry tell it, none of them on the other side was that. I kept on pestering myself with questions like, What about the killing of Tunstall that begun the whole shebang? What about the killing of Dick Brewer and Frank McNabb and Harvey Morris and one-armed Chapman? How about all them that burned out McSween and killed him? Seemed that nothing had changed. Whoever had the power and the money had the right papers to make the law. It made me madder than a bronc with a bee up his butt—couldn't be comfortable nowhere whilst my enemies was now high in the saddle: Dolan, Dudley, Peppin (now retired and safe), Jesse Evans, old man Boyle, Campbell. . . .

And do you know what? I am *still* a wanted man. Sitting right across from you, here in my own house, there's a warrant for my arrest somewheres in that courthouse over in Lincoln. That's a goddamn fact! I had to find this out many years later on when I had finally got Cella to say yes to marrying me, and I went to the courthouse to see the clerk. He was Wade Brewer—cousin to poor old Dick—, and he was checking all the legal matters when he comes across that goddamn outstanding warrant for the Buckshot Roberts business! He comes back to the desk with that raggedy piece of shit in his hand and says to me, 'I don't know about this, Coe. What I ought to do is turn this over to the sheriff, and let him sort it out. It's too much for me.' By Godfrey, what a condition! What was I going to say to Cella after years—*years*—of courting her and trying ever which way to show her I wasn't no outlaw, had changed my sinful ways, and been going to church regular where I'd get down on my goddamn knees and pray God to forgive me for trying to dust them that was trying to do the same to me, and come close to succeeding at Blazer's Mill—.

Well, here. You see the way I still am about this once I get onto the subject. It takes me back to that spring on the Sugarite and what a mean, useless critter I surely was then. And I may say here that except for Frank, I have never told a soul about that warrant, which Wade Brewer, bless him, just kind of buried somewheres and forgot about so Cella and me could get married. I have always thought he done me that favor on account of what happened to Dick at Blazer's Mill, but naturally I never asked. But now, if you was to go on and tell about this to another, why, I would call you a liar to your face.

*

Now, where was I? Oh, yes, unhappy as hell, up on the Sugarite. Well, it was about a year since I'd run across Hendry, and one morning, pulling on my boots, which I didn't even bother to saddle soap no more, I was tugging and swearing at them. Then I stood up, stomping myself into them, already mad and the day just commenced. Frank was looking at me steady. So, I say, 'Well, *what?*'

'Son,' he says, 'you got to change your ways.'

I knew he was right, even before he finished. I was as useless up there as tits on a boar, and there wasn't nothing left for it but to go to Lou and Al and tell them that my time with them was up. They said that when I felt better to come on back, but that this was best for now. 'When you need us, here's family,' was the way Lou put it. Even such a sorry son of a bitch as I was then could appreciate a remark like that. That very afternoon I was saddled up and ready to go, and the three of them stood there in the yard to say goodbye, which put me in mind of saying goodbye to my Pa back in Missouri with the wind blowing hard but a good horse under me. Now I had another good one, maybe better than old Chunk: Mud was a clay-bank dun, mostly mustang, that could stay on a trail long as you could sit him. So then it was just Mud and me, hitting south out of the cold and some late snow here and there.

No one had asked where I was bound for, maybe on account of they knew I had no good idea. I sure wasn't going near Lincoln County, but other than that I only wanted to put some distance between myself and where I had been so miserable. For a ways, I followed the Canadian, camping here and there. One day I had some luck when I come out of the trees at the edge of a meadow, and there was a young doe, nibbling away and not being so wary. She sort of had her tail towards me, so I couldn't get a good broadside shot but still managed to hit her in the ribs, and she run off across the meadow with Mud and me in pursuit. But I could tell from the way she run, sort of crazy-like, that I had hit her pretty good, and just at the meadow's edge, where I begun to fear I might lose her in the woods, she turned and run along the edge, and then I had a good view, and my third shot dropped her. This give me a supply of meat for some days, the weather being still cold enough so that keeping it wasn't a problem.

I went along this way—might have been a couple of weeks—, zigzagging back and forth but not making any true progress in any one direction, and I wasn't truly set up to be one of them mountain men like they used to tell of, all dressed in furs and skins and loaded with traps and guns and such, even if there still had been a market for pelts, which there wasn't. If you're wondering if I was lonesome out there, I guess the answer would be yes, on account of one day I seen I'd been drifting in a general direction towards Las Vegas and so begun to think I might put up there, get a couple of hot meals, a soft bed, and have Mud looked after. As I was thinking this way, I come to a small village on the Mora and in the middle of it a fair-sized church. In front of the church was a hitching post and an old man there trying to mount a heavy-loaded mule. He had all kinds of things hanging off that animal, such that you could hardly see anything of it except the head and legs. One of the things appeared to be some sort of ladder, and it was this the old feller was having a time swinging his leg over. I come off the trail, and as I got close to him I seen his legs just quivering, and as he tried yet again I got down, come up behind him, and give him a good boost. Up he went. He made some adjustments up there in the saddle, saying nothing, but then looked down on me, dropped the reins, and put his hands together like you might if you was praying in a church. I never will forget my first look at that face: it was dark and lined and pitted like it had been hacked out of old wood a long time ago, but the eyes wasn't old at all. They was so dark and sparkly they was almost fierce. It was like they didn't go with the face they was in—except they did.

'Well, old-timer,' I come out, 'you all set up there?'

'I am,' he says and makes that praying sign again. 'Thank you.' He patted his near leg and says, 'Some of these days my legs are not so good.' He smiled, and all them lines run even deeper. But instead of moving along he just sat there, looking down on me with that smile, and so finally I asked him where he was headed to, and he gestured behind him, south. 'Las Vegas,' he says.

'Me, too,' I says. 'Old Mud here needs tending to, and I could stand a bit of that myself.'

'Come along, then,' he says, 'and we will ride there together.'

His name was Juan Nepomuceno Galvez, and he was going to change my life—though of course I couldn't have known that then. But right quick I did know this much, riding next to him on the trail to town: he had some peculiar effect on me, which to this minute I can't put the proper words to. If I give it any thought at the time—which I probably didn't—I might have thought it was just that suddenly I had human company for the first time in many a day. Your horse can be a companion, and I had reason to admire

Mud and be glad for his company. But still, he ain't human, though later I had to shoot him and bury him and grieve him, too. And it wasn't the same thing as taking that first drink of a day, where you feel different all of a sudden and things seem sharper and more lively. Nor was it his talk, for we hardly said twenty words along our way. I have told this story a good number of times down the years since that day, and ever time I do, I get the feeling I'm letting old Galvez down some way, that my telling of how I felt when around him don't nearly come up to the condition itself. And ever time I try it yet again I am hopeful that I'll get it right, or, anyway, edge a bit closer. But I already see this ain't the day.

Anyway, at the outskirts of town we come upon a bunch of Mex horsemen there in the middle of the road, all jabbering and waving and their horses dancing about, and we had to stop. Old Galvez asked them in Mexican what they was so worked up about, and they come back with a long answer, interrupting each other plenty, and I didn't get none of it except 'El Chivato,' and I knew what that meant all right but didn't let on. When Frank and me had said our goodbyes to the Kid outside Anton Chico I determined right there that I was never again going to let on that I knew anything about him other than what someone was telling me when his name come up. Amongst many other things about that young man that you wanted to ride wide of, that was one: safer to pretend you knew him only by his reputation. So when the Mexes had finished with their story old Galvez thanked them in his polite style, and we rode on towards town. After some minutes I begun to wonder if he was never going to tell me what all that was about, and so I asked.

'El Chivato—the Kid—has killed four men and broken out of jail. They say he is coming this way.'

That was the first day of May, eighteen-eighty-one.

When that news come, Pat Garrett wasn't nothing more than a name to me. I knew he was sheriff and had captured the Kid over by Stinking Springs, but the possemen involved in that was a good deal more familiar to me than Garrett, and I think this might have been kind of the general condition hereabouts, so to put it. Folks over in the eastern parts of the territory and in west Texas knew him. But he hadn't had no part whatever in the war, hadn't taken no sides, didn't have no enemies over this way, nor many friends, for that matter. When Chisum was looking about after the war for somebody to run for sheriff, I think these was the things made him settle on Garrett: he didn't have no black marks to work off, like everbody else. Later on, of course, after the Kid was dead, I came to hear more about him, most of it from Doc Blazer and Jim East, who had rode with him in some important actions, and then I met Garrett himself a time or two over here at Eagle Creek. But that was just to shake hands and say howdy and didn't amount to nothing at all. I ain't the sort of feller that goes about telling strangers he knew Pat Garrett on the strength of that, and if it hadn't been a business scheme that brought him my way, what I have to say on this subject of Garrett and the Kid would be about like the feller wants to tell you all about the automobile without knowing about Mr. Ford.

Mind, Garrett didn't know everthing about the Kid; far as that goes, I could have told him things about the Kid he wouldn't have had no way of knowing. But he knew the Kid in ways nobody else did, and I heard a lot of this when we was water prospecting together for two days around here. So you put that together with what I been telling you, and it makes for a fuller picture. But, like I said earlier, it ain't the complete picture—can't be. With the Kid there's always something left out.

*

When Garrett and me was riding around the valley here, he was prospecting for a bunch formed to build an irrigation system that would bring in more farmers and ranchers. He was real worked up about this, and the way he talked, it sounded like a good idea. Maybe it was. But somehow, by the end of that first day things seemed to have soured for him. It was spring—March, maybe—, and so the day was changeful and had begun to snow a bit. By the time we got back to my place it was coming down like winter, and we put up the horses, come in here, and got the stove going. He had got very silent by then, and sitting right where you are now he spit at the stove and hit it. It sizzled, like it was talking back at him, and he said something under his breath I didn't catch. I got down the jug, thinking to jollify him a bit as he was known to like his whiskey. They say an Irishman is like that—Jimmy Dolan was, and died young of it. Murphy, too.

He was some long, lanky feller, tallest man I ever knew.

Everthing about him was that way—hair, moustache, hands, feet: long and tough as old wire. By nature he was a bloodhound. Set him on a trail, he don't give up till he's come up on you. While it's snowing, or raining, or hotter than hell, or nightfall, whatever the conditions, old Pat was a-coming on and a-coming on, even if all his men wanted to call it quits. It's what made him successful where others wasn't. That and courage, which he had—even his enemies have to give him that much. But a bloodhound that's good for one thing ain't suited to another. He ain't really set up to be a yard dog on a chain: that way he gets to feeling useless, and after a bit he can turn mean on you. I found this out about myself up on the Sugarite when I was feeling useless, and I seen a bit of this in him sitting right next to this stove in that late snowstorm.

He was said to be from Louisiana and to have married down there, but somehow when he turned up on the buffalo range in Texas he didn't have a wife nor children, and the story went he had left them behind in Louisiana. Them days of the seventies was about the last of the big herds, and as this was becoming known there was a scramble to get out there and hunt while there was still hunting to do. Teams would go out of a morning, the shooters with their Sharps and tripods, and the knife men, and they might harvest fifty or sixty buff on a good day, so they say: wap off the hides, take the tongues and hump meat, and go along like that, long as the animals was plentiful in that spot, which could be longer than you'd think, on account of what you might call the fatal peculiarity of the beast: when you dropped one, the others might glance over to find out what had happened, but then go right back to grazing, moving on steady. True, sometimes the leaders would bolt at the first shot, but, like I say, more often they'd go right on grazing while the shooters and teams would go on with their deathly work. They could make good money at that, but at the same time they was putting themselves out of business, which is why so many of them ended up working as cowboys or farmers or bronc-busters or bartenders or stock detectives. Garrett himself was looking for some other sort of work when he come across Pete Maxwell, who happened to be short a couple of hands and hired him on the spot. I guess he was a good enough hand for Pete to keep him on several years, but there come a time when they got crosswise, as will happen, and Garrett quit and ended up tending bar for Beaver Smith at old Fort Sumner. That's where folks got to know him and something about him. But a good deal more come out, not while he was alive, but after he was murdered. A famous feller becomes better known, seems like, in the way he dies than in how he become famous. The murder happened on a lonesome road outside of Roswell: he was down off his wagon taking a piss when he got drilled in the back of the head. The man who was with him at the time, name of Brazell, turned himself in and claimed self-defense, which hardly seems likely: hard to defend yourself when your enemy has his pecker in his hand, his back to you, and his shotgun— loaded with birdshot—up on the wagon seat. Anyway, Brazell was acquitted and then disappeared, and to this day nobody knows the true story there, but it's said to be somewhat unhealthy yet to go around certain places, asking questions about it. You still hear some people say that whoever was the killer was avenging the Kid. Maybe that was Brazell or maybe it was another that was there working with Brazell.

However, back to Garrett when he was behind the bar at Beaver Smith's. That wasn't no hog ranch, but it was rough enough, and a bartender in that sort of place has got to be as rough and ready as his worst customer, and has got to have a good head as well. He's got to keep matters somewhat under control at all times, and if he can't, he'll be out of work quick: a saloon can become nothing but a bunch of boards real fast. Garrett could do all these things, and it didn't hurt none that he was said to have killed a man around a campfire back in his Texas days.

It was at Beaver's that he met Charlie Bowdre, Jesse Evans, Fred Waite and where he met the Kid, too. And maybe you heard how those two become pards and went into rustling for a time. I don't know about that part of it, except that the way things finally turned out between them, this makes it a hell of a good story. Generally, though, the truth—whatever that may be—makes the best story I have found, on account of you can't make up a lie that's more tail-twisted than the truth. Here, as far as the Kid and Garrett is concerned, I don't have to make it so that they was pards in order to make it into a grand story. The Kid wasn't a saloon type nor the pardner type, neither, as I've said previous. He was somewhat sociable, but there was just a something that set him apart that way, something that made you keep your distance and respect his. But, in that bartender sort of way, Garrett knew the Kid well enough and was to get to know him even better later on.

*

By the time he come over here on that irrigation scheme he had been famous for many years on account of the Kid. He killed others as well, how many nobody has kept good count. He was a lawman, sure, but he was known as a lawman who killed when he judged he had to. That's why he knew the president of the country, had shook hands with him, and Teddy Roosevelt thought enough of him to give him a job with the government. There's not many can say as much. For quite some years, Garrett could charge a dollar to sign his name, and there was times when he needed that dollar, as he appears not to have had much of a head for business: tried a good many things—cattleman, stock detective, mine operator, racing horses—and failed at most. So by the time our trails crossed I would have to judge him as a bitter man and a bored one as well. This feller had wronged him in some deal; that one he should never have trusted; another had made misjudgments that cost Garrett money he never got back. And beneath all that talk of bad business luck—any man can have that, I guess—was his boredom. There just didn't seem to be nothing in life as interesting to him as hunting down a man and bringing him in—or killing him, if that was needful.

Nowadays, with all this stuff they got in books and the moving pictures, they make that look like it was a game, but them days being a lawman wasn't no play-dolly deal. It was goddamn dangerous work you didn't look to get rich at if you was honest, which I believe Garrett mainly to have been. And you didn't get much thanks for it, neither. You made as many enemies as you did friends—more, I'd say, with folks carrying long memories of pardners or family members you sent to jail or crippled or killed. And then, of course, there was the business of the Kid who had a great many friends, and who continued to gather more friends the longer he stayed dead: people who didn't know a thing about the war (or about the Kid, for that matter) but who come to heroize the Kid and talked about what a cowardly thing Garrett done: shooting him down in the dark when he was carrying only a knife he was fixing to carve himself a steak with for his supper. And there was still other men, not even enemies, really, but who was going around thinking they could get themselves a big reputation by killing the man who'd killed the Kid; or, even better, by making Garrett take water and like it. And he was *such* a target—Garrett, I mean—, looking like he did. He couldn't go nowheres, not even up to Washington, without everbody whispering, 'There goes Pat Garrett, that killed Billy the Kid.'

I don't know that you could say that killing the Kid was the high point of his life, but that thought come to me, on account of how he kept coming back to the Kid while we rode around, though I have to admit that after a few times of him talking that way it was easy enough for me to joggle him with a question about it. Sometimes he would answer and sometimes not, and some other times he would turn back to that question quite a bit later, like he'd been considering it while we was calling on my neighbors. Maybe his mind wasn't *ever* truly on his business, but was always back there in them long ago days, chasing bad men, outthinking them, outlasting them. Might be part of why he wasn't successful with anything else he tried his hand at.

I doubt he ever would have been a lawman if John Chisum hadn't come to him out of nowhere, so to say, telling him if he would run for sheriff, he'd win. He did what Chisum said and won, handy. 'They told me straight off I was to arrest the Kid,' he said, 'but, hell, everbody knew that what they wanted was for me to kill him—Chisum, Catron, them big boys up in Santa Fe, maybe even the governor after a while. Last thing any of them wanted was the Kid up there on the witness stand. He knew *way* too much for that. But them days, wanting a man dead wasn't unusual and was maybe easier on all concerned, except the wanted man, of course. Ewell Richert, that had been a lawman almost twenty years when I met him in Tascosa, told me when I was up for sheriff that from a lawman's standpoint, dead was better than alive. "You'll find," he said, "that it's a good deal more tricky to collect your money if you arrest your man and manage to bring him in alive. There's all kinds of things you never thought of that gets between your delivery and your reward. Whereas, the other way, if you deliver the body, you say, 'Here's the body. Give me my money.'"

'Well, when old Ewell told me this I hadn't learned nothing yet about what they wanted done in the job. Chisum give me advice on how to run, who to talk to, but nothing about what I'd have to do once I won, neither him nor any of the others was backing me. But right after I won—and before I was even legally sheriff—, why, they told me, all right: "Garrett, get the Kid—pronto."

'At that point things was complicated. The Kid was on the loose, had been since the Chapman killing, and him and his boys was cutting into the Jingle-Bob herds pretty regular, as well as the herds of other Seven Rivers ranchers. Wallace was new as governor, didn't know the territory at all, and less than a hill of beans about the war, except maybe what he'd been told up in Santa Fe. And there was some things about it that maybe wasn't necessary for him ever to hear about. And while he's trying to sort things out, here Chapman gets killed right outside the courthouse, so Wallace quick sees what a mare's nest he has come into. He goes down to Lincoln to see for himself what this is all about, and after a few days he does what any sensible man might do in that fix: he puts a cork back in that dark jug of rot that was the war, and issues a general amnesty to all that took part in it. There was a few exceptions there, especially the Kid who he had been told had killed Brady and Hindman and most likely Chapman, too.'

If Garrett ever made up his mind on who killed Chapman, he never said it to me. But at the time, coming in as sheriff, the important thing was not what *he* thought but what the *governor* thought, and Wallace had been told by somebody or somebodies that the Kid done it, so that's what Garrett had to act on, that and the killings of Brady and Hindman. These made the Kid the most wanted man in the territory and the top of Garrett's list of chores to get done.

'I knew him, sure,' Garrett said. 'Everbody knows that. If you ever met him, he stayed in your mind, more so than many a man you'll meet across the bar. Unusual looking, smaller than many and with peculiar eyes that always reminded me of a goat's. Hard to put it another way; they wasn't white like a goat's can be but a light, light gray. And while they was steady, they didn't appear to be looking right at you but looking straight *through* you. Like I say, that made him stand out to you where other men's eyes was common enough—brown, black, blue, red. But as I think back on him—as I have had to do, considering how things come out—I wonder was he ever *really* looking at you? I mean, looking at *you*, the you that your wife sees, or that you see in the mirror. When I had him in custody after Stinking Springs and had a chance to watch him from that different angle, that's when them no-color eyes come to make a kind of sense they hadn't before. What I come to realize by looking at them was that here was a real dangerous little man that would kill you quicker'n you could blink in order to get loose. You wasn't a person—you wasn't George Coe or Pat Garrett or anybody, really. You was just a *thing* that stood between him and what he wanted. I never could get that across to my deputies that was charged with guarding him.'

Coming on the job, one thing that looked a bit favorable for him, Garrett said, was that the Kid had lost some manpower—Frank McNabb, us Coes, Jim French, Fred Waite, Hendry Brown. But still he had some hard characters riding with him, and Garrett knew well enough the Kid wasn't about to become peaceable and settle down. 'He was set in his ways,' is how he put it to me, 'and was bound to live by the long rope, at the monte tables, with his gun, if it come to that. I didn't have no doubt of that, and so there wasn't no point in my kind of letting things be and hoping the Kid would just sort of fade away, maybe go down into Old Mexico. I hadn't been elected to do that; I'd been hired to get him, and that's what my mind was on, right from the start. Now, it's true, there was a point where the Kid might have been willing to testify for Wallace if it could have been worked out, but then there come the Chapman thing, and so that time had passed. And Wallace himself at some point might have been willing to include the Kid in some sort of amnesty, but we'll never know about that, on account of after Chapman all the bets was off. But once, way afterward, I come across Wallace up in Washington, and we got to talking things over, as you will, and he told me that when he met the Kid at Squire Wilson's he was surprised at what a mannerly and likeable fellow he was. And he was that way, too, when the occasion called for it. But there was other things in that boy that was deathly.'

*

The hunt begun quick, right after the election, when word come to Garrett that the Kid and his bunch was up to White Oaks with some horses and was thought to be taking them west to sell at Tascosa. Garrett flang together what he could in the way of a posse and rode hard for White Oaks but was too late—the Kid had gone. He took on some more possemen there though, including the blacksmith, Jim Carlyle. Turned out that only Carlyle was worth anything, the rest being full of shit, and at the worst possible moment they was to run off, leaving Garrett with but three men. But that was a bit later, and at first there was a good deal of big talk when they picked up the Kid's trail outside town and easily followed it in the snow. After some miles Carlyle rode up alongside Garrett and said he pretty well knew where the outlaws was headed; said it had to be the Greathouse ranch.

Whiskey Jim Greathouse is long dead, and there ain't so much as a single board left of his old place, but back in that time he was well known to be a man who worked along both sides of the fence, so to say: he run a place where you could put up for the night, have your horse seen to, and if you happened to be driving some stock you was anxious to be rid of, Greathouse would take them off your hands and not ask troublesome questions about how you come by them. When Garrett and them got near the place, he divided his men up and sent some around to the corrals behind so there couldn't be no escape and told them to fire a shot when they was all in place, which was done. Then he fired another off. Pretty soon here come a holler from the house. 'I said I was Sheriff Pat Garrett,' he told me, 'and I recall it sounded strange to say it that way as I had never had to say it out loud like that—hollering across the snow and all. Anyway, whoever was in the house asked what was wanted, and I said we was there to talk about them horses out back and wasn't leaving until we was satisfied on the matter.' After a bit another man hollered that if Garrett would send a man, they would send out one of theirs, and there could be a discussion that way—it was kind of a hostage swap. So, the exchange was made, with Whiskey Jim coming out to parley, and Carlyle going to the house to tell the Kid they was surrounded and had an hour to surrender.

What happened after this is one of them mysteries we'll never get to the bottom of. But the long and short of it is that when the hour passed, some fool of a White Oaks posseman behind the house fired off a shot, and Jim Carlyle broke away from the outlaws, and jumped through a window, trying to escape. He was shot several times and killed, and then the Kid and his bunch busted out the back, firing, and them coward White Oaks men run off from the outlaws. That left Garrett with but three men, and a popular feller dead in the snow. Nobody knows who killed Carlyle—might be both the outlaws and the possemen, as he was caught in a crossfire. Down to this very day, you can stir up a hell of ruckus in any bar from Portales to Mesilla by claiming you know who killed Jim Carlyle.

Whoever it was, the whole thing didn't do Garrett's reputation no good, him having the Kid surrounded, then letting him get away and losing a valuable man into the bargain. But yet, he was all the more determined to get the Kid, judged he had him on the run, and that if he could just get some men riding with him who would stand their ground, he would get his man. Shortly, he did get some, too: Lon Chambers, Barney Mason, Jim East, and Ted Blasingame. When he got them together, he told them that if they was to ride hard and not give up, they could have the outlaws in their sights come Christmas. The trail led to Fort Sumner.

VII

You had to be a tough hombre to ride with old Pat, and these new fellers was all of that, including Barney Mason, who many didn't care for but was a hard man when it counted. I knew Jim East fairly well. Later on, he become a sheriff himself; seen a good deal in his day, and knew quite a bit about the Kid, though he weren't at all the kind to go around bragging. He was with Garrett and the rest when they learned a few days before Christmas that the Kid and his bunch was hiding out on a ranch east of Sumner. Word was they was in the habit of going in to Beaver Smith's at night for entertainment, and so one night Garrett laid an ambush for them at the old Indian hospital where Manuela Bowdre was staying. He figured them to drop Charlie off to see her and then go on to Beaver's.

It had turned so almighty cold on the way there that Garrett had to keep whipping up even these tough men to keep on going, telling them they could soon get warmed up in one of the hospital rooms that had a fireplace, and that's the way it turned out: they got in out of the cold, built a good fire, thawed out, and spread a blanket on the floor to play poker on. Except Lon Chambers: he drew the short straw and Garrett posted him along the road their targets would have to come in on. They hadn't been settled long when Chambers come running in and said riders was approaching. 'Boys,' Garrett told them, 'there can't be nobody else out in this weather this late: these are our men.'

They took up their positions and heard the horses before they could see them: there was a moon up but with a low fog as well. Garrett and Mason was on the portal, hiding in the shadows behind an old plow horse harness and some ristras. Garrett remembered the lead horseman was damn near under the portal before they made him out. Said, 'I could have reached out and touched his horse's muzzle when he reined in.

'"Hands up!" I says, and he jerked back to turn his horse around, but didn't make it: I fired on him, and hit him in the chest. He screamed out, got his horse turned, and then the rest of my men let go. That was where the fog come in handy for the outlaws: you could only get off but one good shot before they disappeared up the road, and I was left cursing and thinking, "Well, *shit!*—maybe we only got one, if that."

'I had just stepped out from the portal when here come a lone horseman back out of the fog, slumped on his horse's neck. I had my gun on him, but when he spoke I knew I didn't need it, on account of he was coughing blood. "Don't shoot," he says to me, "I'm killed." It was Tom O'Folliard. I believe it was Barney who grabbed the horse's bridle, and we got Tom down. He had clamped his teeth down but was bleeding quite a lot through them anyways and was spotting the snow when we carried him in and laid him on the blanket next to the fire. That messed up our cards, but then, we wasn't playing for much. I ain't going to go into what all he said to me whilst he was dying, things about my wife and my mother and whatnot. They was rough to listen to, but if you've shot a man and know he's going to die, I believe you're bound to hear him out. After a time, Tom asked for a drink of water, and when it was given, he threw it up with a lot of blood and died.'

The next morning Garrett found some fellers to hack a hole in the ground, and they laid O'Folliard in it, as both Frank and Hendry had predicted would happen.

*

Well, sir, now Garrett had them on the run, like he'd told his new posse he would, and a bloodhound in that condition, you can't get him off the trail unless you intend to use force, and wasn't nobody about to do that with Pat Garrett, especially them big boys that had put him up to it in the first place. The trail took them east from Sumner, and at first it was plain enough, but then it commenced snowing again and blowing hard, too, and by the time they passed by the Wilcox place they had lost it and just halted there, stumped. They all knew there wasn't nothing beyond there for a good stretch except an old rock hut used long ago by sheepherders. Called it Stinking Springs on account of the creek that run below it had sulfur in it. Garrett could feel the heart going out of his men, who was all for turning back to Sumner. Not the bloodhound, though. He asked if anybody knew where the rock hut lay from where they now was, and when Lon Chambers said he thought he could find it, Garrett said he was bound to investigate that place.

They went on through the snow that was beginning to be heavy going for the horses. Near dark Chambers saw a landmark he knew and judged they was close, and Garrett called a halt. If there was men up ahead in the hut, there must be horses, and these are such sociable creatures, like to talk to their kind. So, they went the rest of the way on foot. When they could make out the hut, they seen horses tethered to the vigas. But no sound nor even smoke come from inside. Garrett sent some men up above to a little clump of mesquite while he and the others was down in an arroyo. Then they settled in to wait for dawn. It was another bitter night, and as they was so close to the hut there was to be no fires, no talking, not even slapping your hands together to get your fingers warmish.

'I reminded all of them,' Garrett said, 'that the Kid customarily wore a sugarloaf hat with a green band, and if they was to see such a man, they was to fire on him without warning. But when it come first gray and I could see the horses good, I didn't see that roan amongst them and thought again, "Well, *shit!* We ain't got him yet—they've split up." But not long after, we heard noises from the hut that told us they had a horse or two crowded in there with them for the warmth. Then, out come a man in a sugarloaf hat and carrying a nosebag for his horse, and I fired on him directly. Others followed, but I could tell my bullet had got home on account of he swung right around and went as if to go back inside but hit the jamb, and his hat fell off. Somebody inside reached out and pulled him through while the hat stayed out there in the snow. It had a green band, all right, but then I heard the Kid's voice among the others and knew I'd got the wrong man—an outlaw, all right, but not the Kid. We fired a few more shots at the hut, but then stopped, listening to the shouting from inside.

'Then the door opened, and a man without a hat come out, but it would be more truthful to say he was shoved out. It was Charlie Bowdre. He had a big old Colt Navy cap-and-ball pistol in his fingers, but he wasn't going to hurt nobody with it. It was just dangling there off his hand whilst he staggered towards us. He was a dead man, sure, and how he kept coming was a wonder, but when he got to the bank of the arroyo he missed his step and pitched down to where I was, and I caught him and laid him down easy. He was trying to talk, but I couldn't make out what he wanted to say, so I put my face down to his to ask what it was.

'"I wish," is all he said, just that—"I wish." And you know how when you say "wish" you got to kind of blow your wind out to make the word? Well, Charlie done that way, and that breath out—that hit me right in the face and was his last in this world—you got any more in that jug back at your place, Coe?'

At that point we was well into our second day of water prospecting and had intended to call on some people between San

Patricio and my place, but here Garrett was signaling he was done for the day—the same man who wouldn't ever quit on a trail and had gone through snow and night to investigate that rock hut. It took me by surprise, but we changed our directions right there, and when we was back at my place I give him a pretty good jolt, which he took down quick and then give a long belch, like he'd tasted something bad, though just the night before he hadn't made no objections to my whiskey. But, what he said then hadn't nothing to do with what he was drinking: it was that in them last two days he'd been telling me of, he had killed two men—ended *everthing* for them—, and neither one was the man he was really after. Plus, he had a fair opinion of Charlie and had reason to believe he was intending to quit the Kid and go straight, as Manuela had been after him to do. And on top of that, her and Garrett's wife was quite friendly.

He set there silent quite a spell with them long legs stretched out and his chin on his chest, holding the glass with both hands. Somehow, you don't want to bother a man in that condition, especially that particular man. I ain't the sort that is accustomed to go kowtowing to somebody just because he happens to be famous, but still, this was *Pat Garrett*, for Christ's sake, sitting there at my stove, looking gray and spent all of a sudden. It would give *you* a pause, too, pardner, had you been in my boots. So, I busied myself doing something or other that didn't need doing, and while I was rattling around that way I heard him speaking in a low voice, and damn if he hadn't gone back to the killing of Charlie.

'When Charlie give it up,' he was saying, almost like to himself, 'I searched amongst his clothing for the fatal wound and found it, just under the rib cage on the left side. Bullet might have hit bone and then traveled up to the heart, as there was quite a bit of blood. And while I was at this, I come upon something else: in his vest old Charlie was carrying a picture of him and Manuela that was all covered with his heart's blood, which I had shed.'

He looked across at me when saying this, putting me in mind somehow of the way a big sky can look when it's fixing to storm on you, and there ain't no shelter in sight—no forgiveness there.

'I quick pulled it out and blotted it best I could on my sleeve, and give it to Barney Mason to hand on to Manuela; under proper circumstances I would have done that myself, but these was hardly the proper ones. Then, I hollered to the hut that Charlie was dead and that there was no need for further men to die, as we had them surrounded and was well prepared to wait till they come out. It was the Kid's voice come back, laughing, and telling me what we could do with our guns; said they had guns, too, and was in shelter where we wasn't. "We'll wait till we hear your peckers freeze off, Pat," he says, and so forth.'

Well, there wasn't nothing for them to do then but wait 'em out. There was but one window to the hut and that was boarded up, and the door, and as there wasn't no smoke coming out Garrett judged they'd gone in there for the night without bothering to collect firewood and only the horses inside for heat. He ordered some men to gather some mesquite branches for a big fire and sent another man back to the Wilcox ranch for bacon and beans and feed for the horses, and then, so he said, 'We had all the best of it: we had a fire—and you know how hot mesquite burns—, and after a while we had our meat and beans and coffee a-cooking, whilst them inside didn't have nothing but the smells of our plenty. The Kid, he kept up his smart talk, and I kept asking if he could use some breakfast. "When are you going to kill that fine roan I know you got in there, Kid?" I says, "and have yourself a good steak—raw?" He come back smart again, but then there wasn't nothing from them. But I'll tell you, that smell of beans and bacon and coffee—pardner, if you're inside a rock hut in winter and freezing your tail off, that can be a powerful draw.'

Midafternoon, Garrett seen the door crack and a man make a grab at the reins of the nearest of the tethered horses to pull him inside, but Garrett stopped that operation quick. 'I shot that animal in the neck,' he said, 'and he dropped like a meal sack, right blocking the door, so they was further buffaloed if their notion was to mount up in there and come busting out. Less than an hour after that the door cracked open again, and a crooked bit of iron with a torn white cloth come out, and a voice said, "We give up, providing you don't shoot."

'"Let me hear it from the Kid,"' Garrett says, and then the Kid come back and said they'd had enough and was willing to settle for some grub and a fire. The terms was, horses out first, then the Kid with his guns throwed ahead of him; then a ten-count between each man following, until all was out. Any kind of misstep and the posse was to commence firing until all was down, horses as well as men.

Out jumped the roan over that dead horse in the doorway, but then there was trouble with the second horse that was spooked by the dead one, but finally they got him out. Then the Kid flang out his .41 and the Winchester and come out smiling and asked Garrett if he could pick up his hat, and Garrett said go ahead. But just as he reached down, Barney Mason hollered out, 'Let's kill the little son of a bitch while we got him dead to rights.' Said the Kid was a treacherous bastard that couldn't be trusted under any conditions. But Jim East and Blasingame cracked down on Barney and said if he shot, they'd kill him, and that ended that. The rest come out peaceable—Wilson, Rudabaugh, Tom Pickett. Garrett gave them a quick bite to eat, and then they started to Sumner with Charlie tied up behind Jim East.

When they got there and went to Manuela's room in the old hospital, why, she went just crazy. She kicked and clawed Garrett like a wildcat, until somebody pulled her off, and then she turned on Jim East who was carrying the body and bashed him over the head with a fire poker. Garrett judged that if East hadn't been wearing a heavy, high-crowned hat, she'd have killed him.

'As it was,' he said, 'Jim dropped the body, which made a bad sound, as it was froze pretty hard, and Manuela fell on it and wouldn't let nobody near it.' There's a story that Garrett paid for a new suit to bury Charlie in. He never said that to me, but I believe it. It would be like him to buy the suit and not go around bragging about it.

There's another story that goes along with the capture, one Garrett never said nothing about to me, or anybody else, near as I can figure. This one I didn't believe for many a year, for a couple of reasons. First, it sounded like one of them stories that seemed to kind of crowd around anything to do with the Kid—like flies on a bacon rind, so to say. You know how they go: Jack told Mack and Mack told Zack. After a time, it comes to be the truth, and you can't get rid of it. You just have to live with it, even if you never truly believe in it. The story had it that when the posse had got back to the old hospital with the prisoners, dead and alive, Garrett allowed the Kid to go into another room to say goodbye to his girlfriend, Paulita Maxwell, Pete's younger sister, on account of the next morning they was taking him and the others up to the jail at Las Vegas. That right there is the reason I never believed the story: Pat Garrett would *never* have let a prisoner as important as the Kid go anywhere, unless guarded, even to the shitter. But I kept on hearing that story, until finally one day I heard it from a reliable man. Name was Lee Hall, and he was present. But it was the way Hall told it made all the difference: Garrett *did* let the Kid go in to Paulita—but he was shackled to Dave Rudabaugh and guarded by Jim East.

The thing here that's worth considering is that by then Garrett had figured out how special Paulita was to the Kid, amongst all them other gals, and this bears hard on that night in eighty-one in Pete Maxwell's bedroom at Sumner when the Kid come to the end of his trail. With him dodging and running in them last days and Garrett breathing hard on him, the very last place the

Kid would have been figured to hide out was back at Sumner where Paulita was staying. But right here's where he outfoxed Garrett, going to the place that would be the most dangerous one possible, figuring Garrett would right away cross it off his list just because it was so dangerous. So, in a way, for the Kid, Sumner really was almost perfect. Only place better would have been across the border down into Old Mexico.

*

Well, now Garrett had the man he'd been elected to get and said his first thought was getting the Kid and the others the hell out of Sumner and up to the jail at Las Vegas quick as possible. He put it to me this way: 'A lawman often enough don't know just how dangerous his man is until he's got him prisoner. He knows what crimes his man has done, but what he don't know until he has him in irons is what that man is capable of doing to get free of them irons. And the feller that taught me that lesson was the Kid.

'I begun learning from him on our way up to Vegas when I could watch him close, and while he was in Vegas I got to watch him some more. Then, when we had to transfer our prisoners to the train over to Santa Fe, I seen yet some more on this matter: if you had your eyes peeled good, it was a real education.

'What I seen was that there wasn't a single instant when that boy wasn't scheming in his mind to make a break. The others— Rudabaugh and them—was kind of sulky-like: didn't say much, pretty much done what they was told, and looked like they knew they was caught fast. Not the Kid. That whole time he was jolly and talkative, made jokes with his guards and the jailer and a newspaper feller who come to take an interview of him. Made friends with them, too, which is my point here: he was trying to figure a way he might use them in a getaway, how they might do something for him, in a friendly manner—just some little thing—that would give him a sliver of a chance. And this included me. He laughed and joked me, brought up funny things that happened between us at Beaver's, told me I could have the use of that roan he rode, until such time as he was free to ride him again. He had real winning ways to him, and he was showing me all of them. And when we had a spell of trouble at the Vegas depot, where a crowd tried to board the train and take our prisoners out and hang them, the Kid says to me, "Pat, you hand me one of your pistols, and together we'll take care of their business for them." And, you know, there was just a second, flash-like, when I thought about it, as it was a ticklish condition there: we was outnumbered bad, and that crowd was in an ugly mood.

'But then, just as quick, I recollected what I'd been seeing since Stinking Springs: that all the while when he was jollifying the whole town, so to say, them no-color eyes was just a-going and a-going—looking here, looking there, looking around a room. It was like he was calculating what it might take to get him from here to there; where the gun rack was in the jail and how it was kept; what horses was out back—was they getaway horses, or only the fire horses that was pastured there? He was busy, was what he was, and behind that laughing he was *all* business, all of the time. When he was talking with you, his eyes was flittering around, but when they come back to you and rested there a moment, you felt a chill down through you—least I did—on account of that's when you seen that there wasn't *nothing* in this world he wasn't capable of. Nothing.

'In my time as a lawman I've had some pretty desperate hombres in my custody, but never a one come close to the Kid in murderousness, and by the time I turned him over to the federal men in Santa Fe, I had it settled in my mind that if he ever give just the slightest twitch in my presence, I would empty my gun into him quick as I could do it.'

VIII

As is well known, Garrett wasn't around when the Kid finally did make that 'twitch,' and that was what old Galvez and me had heard about when we come into Las Vegas. That was *all* you heard long as you was there, that and the number of men he'd killed in making it. The number kept going up and down but mainly up. You went into a bar, men was jabbering about it in high tones, arguing whether he had been sprung by friends or had tricked the guards, or some other kind of unlikely foolishness altogether. Them days, jailbreaks wasn't uncommon, but this here was a whole different deal—the most famous outlaw in the whole region, in the whole country, maybe—kills his guards and breaks out and just disappears. So, then there had to be sightings of him everwhere you can think of, some of these causing fights where one feller would say he knew for dead certain the Kid had been spotted in some Mex village between Santa Fe and Taos and was riding a gray with a black hind leg, and the other would call him a liar since *he* knew the Kid had gone down into Old Mexico, where he was a guest at a big hacienda near Juarez.

But even all this wasn't enough: there had to be talk as well about the Kid's women, who he was said to be meeting up with here and there, and he would've had to be a two-peckered billy goat in rut to have put it to all the gals they mentioned. So, between all the killings and the fuckings, the Kid was figured as a regular terror let loose on the territory. All this was only what the white men was saying, and I make no doubt the Mexes was up to the same things where they gathered, but if I had gone into them places, I wouldn't have understood none of that without old Galvez along, and I had lost track of him soon as I got to town. Anyway, I didn't figure him as the sort that hung around in bars. That left me pretty much to myself, even though I went to the bars and took my dinners in a café. I probably discouraged conversation by the way I looked at folks that come near to where I was sitting.

After a few days of this I had a bellyful of the Kid this, the Kid that, and judged it might be time to move along. I had other considerations as well. One had to do with the whereabouts of the Kid. It wouldn't have made sense for him to ride into Las Vegas or any other town with Garrett on his trail, but he might well enough have friends hereabouts where he could hide out, and the one thing I didn't look forward to was our trails crossing again, especially now that he was likely more dangerous than ever, if that was possible. Not that I knew that he was out there gunning for George Coe, but I remembered the feeling of thinking he *might* be, from that time when me and Nazarina was down by the river at night, and I didn't ever want to feel that way again, if it could be avoided. The other thing was money. I had saved my wages from up on the Sugarite, but they wasn't going to last me forever, and so me and Mud had to find work before too long.

The thing that caused me to decide that day had come was the two fellers that was bunking in the same boardinghouse as me and who got into it on the porch one morning, just outside my window. I was sleeping off a pretty good drunk, and here these fools was hollering at each other after one called Garrett a coward son of a bitch, and the other come back that if he said such a thing again, he'd knock his teeth back down his throat. Then they commenced to wrestle, slamming into the wall of my room, so there wasn't nothing for it finally but to get up, settle up, and ride out of there quick as I could manage, trying in that way to leave the Kid and all the stories behind me. Big as the territory was, this still wasn't likely, but I had to give it a try.

*

Whatever you want to say about Pat Garrett, you got to leave 'coward' out of it, though if you get famous enough you'll always have somebody who'll say ugly things about you, I don't care who you are. If you're in a bar or such-like, sooner or later some cross-eyed drunk with one leg will tell you Jesus Christ was a Jew, and dare you to say he wasn't. Garrett wasn't a coward when the Kid was on the loose, and wasn't thereafter: the record's plain on that. I don't know where he was when the Kid made his breakout, but I do know it wasn't his job to guard him. He was sheriff, not a guard, and also a deputy U.S. marshal, and had plenty of things that took him all over the county, which you may have noticed is a fair-sized bit of property. In Lincoln, he left two men to guard the Kid, and both had their reasons to make certain he hung right on schedule. J. W. Bell was one of many that was satisfied the Kid had killed his good friend Carlyle. The other was Bob Olinger, who was in the big shootout and claimed he saw the Kid kill his friend Bob Beckwith.

I never met neither man. Bell had a reputation as being a nice enough feller, but like a lot of other matters where the Kid is concerned, this here one of Bell's character has changed a lot, and the longer we get away from when he was alive and guarding the Kid, he gets nicer and nicer to where now he's damn near an angel—makes a better story, you see. Olinger was different—Pecos Bob, as he liked to be called. Some said he was one tough hombre: big, strong, handy with his fists as he was with his gun. Others had it he was nothing but a bully who would be happier shooting a man in the back, rather than face-to-face. Nobody ever said he was nice, even his mother. Everbody agreed he hated the

Kid and could hardly wait for the hangman to do his work. So, here you had these two guarding their sworn enemy that they had chained to the floor upstairs in the courthouse—what used to be the stronghold of the old Firm. When I heard that part of it, it made me madder yet about the way the war turned out and also, suddenly, to feel bad for the Kid, prisoner in the fort of his enemies, who had finally found a safe way to kill him. Maybe the only thing missing would've been to have Dudley himself be the jailer. But Olinger was a good enough substitute, happy as hell to see the fix the Kid was in, chained down like a bronc on hobbles and the clock ticking away to execution day: he could only move about a foot or two either way, or stand by the window and throw down crumbs from his dinner plate for the birds. He did have visitors once in a while but none when Olinger was on duty, as he turned them all away.

Garrett had told me his instructions to the guards, as I mentioned: never give the Kid an inch of leeway; never take your eyes off him when he's near you; when he needs to go to the shitter, go there with him and watch him while he does his business. Still, it's one thing to hate a man and live for the day he dies and another to follow your orders correctly, on account of hatred can make you blind just when you need to be clear-sighted. I mean, if I was to really *hate* you, I ain't seeing what's right there in front of me. Instead, I'm thinking about all the reasons why I hate you and feeling all them things boiling away inside of me and making my eyes red as murder. Meanwhile, there's the *real* you right there in front of me, but I can't see it. That could be dangerous to me if you happened to be a ready killer. I learned part of this lesson when Yginio told me about Kip Brown shooing them chickens away from McSween's eyes outside the burning house: harder to hold fast to your hate for a man who can do that, but you got to let yourself see it. (I was to learn a good deal more along this way of thinking from old Galvez—that come later—, but I never did learn from him all about how to turn the other cheek: for men like me and Frank that lost so much in the war, that's a hard one, pardner—other cheek, my ass!)

I don't know if Bell called himself a Christian, but from what you hear about how he come to treat the Kid, he kind of did turn the other cheek, giving some kindnesses to the man he believed to have killed Carlyle. Olinger wasn't no Christian and treated the Kid like the devil himself, come up on earth. They say he liked to spend his watch telling the Kid how it would be when he hung: how the drop would snap his neck, and that when he made that half-turn at the end of the rope he would shit himself in front of everbody. If Olinger done so—maybe a safe enough guess—, that would make the condition like one devil guarding another. That don't mean I believe *all* of the stuff they tell about what Olinger did to the Kid, though, like that business of what he was supposed to of told the Kid on the day of the breakout while he was loading up his shotgun before going across to dinner: they have him saying that the man that took one of them loads would feel it. And then the Kid was said to have come back, 'Be careful you don't shoot yourself, Bob,' which was in a peculiar way what come to happen. But who would know all this? The only man that survived them minutes after Olinger took some prisoners across to Wortley's for what turned out to be his last supper was the Kid himself. And while it's true this was just the kind of joking he did, I never heard nobody say the Kid said this was how it all happened. So, what I'm giving you here ain't any of these rumors; it's as near the truth as anybody's ever going to get, pardner, and you can count on that.

*

For such a famous event it's remarkable how no one seen the whole of it—except the Kid, of course—, and many an important thing isn't known. Puts me in mind of the Little Big Horn, which at the time was real famous but ain't well understood to this very day. What ain't in question is that by the time hanging day was close Bell had give up on hating the Kid and was doing him them kindnesses that eased his condition some. A man waiting to hang is bound to appreciate whatever is done in that way, and I believe the Kid probably did appreciate it, though in a way different from what Bell had in mind, and was no doubt glad that afternoon when Bell come on watch and Olinger took the prisoners across to Wortley's. Olinger left his shotgun across the hall in Garrett's office but carried his sidearm and a big pig-sticker stuck in his belt that made him look like Wild Bill. But he didn't figure on trouble from his prisoners, as he was known and feared as a man who would shoot to kill at the littlest excuse.

They was just settling in to eat when here come two shots, close together. Olinger jumps up, pulls his sidearm, and quick herds the prisoners outside and warns 'em not to make a move. Then he runs across to the courthouse and around to the side steps that takes you up to the second floor. That was as far as he ever got in this old world, as there was the Kid, up at his window with Olinger's shotgun trained on him steady.

'Hello, Bob,' he says and lets Olinger have both barrels in the face and chest—them same thirty-six buckshot Olinger was supposed to of said a man would feel. Then he goes to hammering the gun against the windowsill till the stock breaks off and flang the pieces down on Olinger, and yelled something at him.

All them across the way at the Wortley seen this, and so did Gauss, a feller done chores at the courthouse and lived out back of it—had him a German-kind of first name I can't now recall—and was once a cook for Tunstall out to the ranch. If anybody ever knew most of what went on in the breakout, it would have been Gauss, though, here again, there was lots he didn't see. Anyways, Gauss later said that what the Kid yelled at Olinger was that he was a yeller son of a bitch. That might have been it, but then, Gauss was interviewed a lot over the years and changed his story around some, as you probably would have to, repeating it so many times.

But what went on upstairs after Olinger left?—that's the real mystery here, and Gauss couldn't answer it on account of he never was inside after Olinger took the prisoners across to the Wortley. What Gauss did see when he looked up from whatever he was working on was the Kid, shuffling along toward the shitter in his leg irons and handcuffs and Bell right behind; Bell had his sidearm, but it was holstered. When the Kid went in and shut the door, Bell was waiting outside and looked over, seen Gauss, and hollered something Gauss didn't catch. So then the two of them walked toward each other to talk. Turned out that what Bell had hollered wasn't nothing but some remark about the weather—fine day or some such. Whilst they was breezing, the Kid come out and started back into the building, and Bell turned to follow him. Gauss said he didn't run but just walked along, fairly smart. When Gauss turned back to his work he heard a shot and then another and then a big commotion from inside, and while he's kind of frozen there, you might say, Bell come out the open door and made some steps as if to commence running, but fell down. That unstuck Gauss, who run over to him and seen he'd been shot right between the shoulder blades but was still breathing. Then he got himself together some and run around the building, hollering to anybody that the Kid had shot Bell. That's when he seen Olinger with his gun out and about to run up them outside steps. And then they both heard the Kid's voice and the *ka-BLAM, ka-BLAM* that was the end of Pecos Bob. The two guards was dead in something inside two minutes by my calculations and both because they didn't follow Garrett's orders.

Gauss didn't need to go over to Olinger to see he was dead, and so he run back to Bell to see if maybe he was still alive, and that's when he heard the Kid calling down to him from a back window, telling him he wasn't going to shoot him and wouldn't have shot Bell only it couldn't be helped. You do what I say, he says, and you'll be all right. Turned out, what he wanted was for Gauss to throw him up a little pickaxe that was lying in the yard next to Bell, and after a couple of tries Gauss gets it up through the window, and hears the Kid going to work on them leg irons.

While all this was going on—not a long spell, mind you—a crowd had gathered across the way, but none had got too close: they could see what become of Olinger, and the word had passed amongst them about Bell. Nobody there wanted any part of that business with the killer somewhere loose in the building. Then here come the killer himself, out onto the balcony where they could see additional reasons to keep their distance: he had two pistols in his waistband and a shotgun that was pointing their way. He had got one leg loose of the irons and had the chain of the other looped up under his belt.

With so many present there was bound to be different accounts of what he said to them, but most recollected that he said he didn't want to have to shoot nobody, but if anybody tried to stop him, that man would die. Then he pointed to one of the prisoners and told him to fetch him a little black horse that was tied up at the hitching post at Wortley's. It belonged to a court clerk and proved to be a mettlesome critter when the Kid tried to mount it with all them chains and guns: the horse bucked him off, and the Kid landed on his ass in the street. So here was a dangerous condition, for certain: him there in the street with the shotgun flang away in the dust, the crowd just feet away, and the two lawmen dead, one of them in plain view with his face shot off.

Them days most carried a sidearm, and there had to be any number in that crowd that could have pulled and shot the Kid, but none did. When you think about it this ain't too surprising, though. What if a man shot and missed or only wounded the Kid?

He'd have been a gone goose is what, and for no good reason: it wasn't his job to make certain the Kid kept his appointment with the hangman but Pat Garrett's. So, nobody stopped the Kid when he got back on the horse and rode west out of town. Several miles along toward what's now Carrizozo there's a big block of stone that juts out into the road so you got to go around it, and that's where a feller name of Sandalio Alvarez met up with the Kid. He didn't recognize who the rider was but really didn't have to: anytime you come across a man on a lonesome stretch of road that has a leg iron and weapons hanging off him ever which way, if you can't hide, you want to make yourself small as possible, which a feller with his mule and wagon full of wood couldn't do. So, he just kind of looked down at his boots and didn't say nothing. Said when the Kid come past he was talking to the little black.

Way later on—years—I learned from Yginio Salazar that the Kid was headed up through the Capitans and down the other side to his place, where Salazar helped him get free of his leg irons. Salazar give him a pretty fair horse, and together they led the little black to where it could see the road back to Lincoln. They give it a good whack on the rump, and away it went. Feller that owned that animal kept it till it died and got a good many drinks out of letting folks ride 'Billy the Kid's horse.'

*

That's as much as will ever be known for a certainty about the breakout, so we're still left with the question we begun with: how in hell did he do it? Folks is still trying to figure that out. For a long time it was said that the Kid and Bell was playing cards, and when the Kid dropped a card on purpose Bell reached down for it, and the Kid quick snatched his pistol from the holster. I even seen a painting a feller did that shows just how that happened. Pretty good picture, but it couldn't have happened so on account of there weren't enough time for them to sit down and go to playing from when Gauss seen them go back inside. Plus this: after the crowd was satisfied the Kid had gone for good, they all rushed upstairs and found the little table where Bell and the Kid used to play. And there was the cards, stacked up neat as ever.

Many others think the Kid got hold of a pistol that had been hid for him in the shitter, and when Frank and me was talking through all this one night when we was supposed to be talking farm business, he said he favored that explanation. The way he reasoned made good sense to me. The Kid had a lot of friends who sure as hell didn't want to see him swing, and so even if chances was slim of him being able to shoot his way past his guards, that would be a better death than what Olinger kept talking about. I never seen a man hung, but if it does happen that way, I would surely rather take my chances with a pistol in my hand instead of swinging with shit in my britches! Once you line things up this way, they make a good deal of sense. For instance, maybe that's why the Kid went right back into the courthouse when he come out of the shitter: he had that gun hid inside his shirt or somewheres and didn't want Bell to see it.

But after thinking about it all through the years, I come to a different conclusion, which was that the Kid had been waiting and waiting for his new friend Bell to make a mistake, even the tiniest one—and this one wasn't tiny: I'm talking about his getting a good head start on Bell going back upstairs, you see. Once he'd got to the top of them steps he slipped one hand out of his bracelets, and when Bell gets up there he uses the bracelet to club Bell and grab his sidearm. He could have slipped his hand out any time, of course, him having the smallest hands I ever seen on a full-grown feller, but he was waiting for that *one* time that would give him the best possible chance, and here it come. He fired twice with Bell's pistol. One was dead center, and that commotion Gauss heard out in the yard was a dead man falling down the stairs.

Some years back I had business that took me to the courthouse, and when I finished with it something come over me I can't explain, except it was like a tap on my shoulder, almost like it was the Kid himself, reaching out and touching me, and telling me to go have a look at his handiwork. So, instead of going on about my other errands, I went up them back steps to the second floor and stood there trying to figure how it could have happened so god-awful quick. Sure, he had that head start on Bell, but you got to remember them leg irons, too. So, I tried picturing him, hopping up that long staircase, one stair at a time, then getting off to one side where Bell couldn't see him, until it was too late and the Kid was on him, clubbing him with the empty handcuff and chain. But picturing all this just so, you still have to have him get hold of Bell's pistol, pull it out of the holster, aim it, and fire twice. Anything that went wrong here—even by a little—, and Bell would have covered him and shot him—ain't no friends nor Christian feelings at that moment, only staying alive. I have to think only the Kid could have done it and then gotten across to get Olinger's shotgun and back to the window in time to line him up in his sights: 'Hel-lo, Bob'— just as he done Frank and me up to Anton Chico.

It is still a wonderment. When I started in trying to tell you about the Kid I knew—his makeup and all—I believe I said he was cold as anything just when it was hottest and that there was a something way down there inside of him that wasn't quite human—, at least not human that I could recognize on account of having seen it in another man. Garrett told me he come to understand at Las Vegas that there wasn't nothing the Kid wasn't capable of in the right conditions. Here in this thing of the break-out, the Kid was able to kill both guards only seconds apart, handcuffed, leg-cuffed, and all, and then buffalo a whole town and make his escape. Maybe that takes a devil to do it, or anyway a something that ain't put together like you and me that have a heart that keeps time with the rest of the world.

149

IX

A s I said when telling you about getting drove out of Las Vegas by all the Kid rumors, me and Mud drifted west through the Cimarron range. Weather was warm, and when I shot another doe I wasn't able to keep much of the meat as it got high after just a few days in my saddlebags. On the other side of Bobcat Pass I come down towards the Red River and near sundown seen quite a bit of smoke ahead. I kept on towards it, then turned uphill a ways so I could look down and see what the conditions might be. Turned out to be a bunch of men and their horses camped in a clearing. They was cooking something around a big fire, and I heard a lot of shouting and laughing. The size of the fire and the way they was carrying on made me judge I probably was safe riding down to them. Coming in to something like that can be dangerous, of course, on account of you don't know what such a bunch will do when a stranger appears in their midst, but I was probably tempted some by the smell of their cooking and made sure I picked out a way that give them plenty of time to spot me. When they did, they got up and one man had his rifle ready, but then they showed themselves friendly enough. There was six of them, five whites and a black feller, and they was kind of cooking huge pieces of beef on sticks—when the piece wasn't too heavy or the stick didn't catch fire. When a feller's meat fell in the fire, they would all holler and make fun of him while he tried to rescue his dinner. The black they called Cap give me a slab of the beef that I cut into a portion I could manage, and so had a good meal helped along by a jug of Taos whiskey they was passing around, one of several they had, as it turned out.

As I mentioned, I had been keeping pretty much to myself since leaving my family up on the Sugarite, all except for them few hours I was in the company of old Galvez. Being around this bunch made me realize why. They was as seedy a bunch as I ever come across, and that takes in some territory, pardner. These boys drank hard all day and lay about in their filth—empty jugs and beef bones just flang everwhere. They didn't bother to go far from the campsite to shit, neither, and you could see a man hanging his ass over a log fifty feet from where you was. That kind of thing will unsettle you considerable. Even their horses didn't look like they'd been seen to in a while, and from the looks of the meadow it had been pretty well grazed out.

One morning they saddled up and rode out, leaving me and Cap there in camp. That made me a bit uneasy on account of I had never talked to a black man before and wasn't minded to now, they being strange to me; also, I was still stuck in that lonesome rut I had been in for quite a spell. Yet he turned out to be not unpleasant. When after a bit I said something to him, he come back mannerly enough. His people had come up out of the South after the Civil War to Kansas where he was raised, and that kind of made him seem less strange, as we had been sort of neighbors without knowing it. How he come to be amongst these fellers he didn't say, but when they come back at dusk it was plain what his job was: they was all packing fresh-killed parts of a cow, and when they unloaded, Cap went to work with a long knife, cutting away the uneatable parts and throwing them in the fire where they crackled and hissed and sent up sparks that made the others laugh while they passed around another jug.

A few days of that was plenty enough for me, and one morning I packed my gear to ride out, not wanting to be a part of their game and judging that, careless as they was, they would soon enough be found out by whoever's cows they was shooting. I didn't want to be amongst them when that occurred. When I was mounted and ready they all stood around, scratching their asses and wiping their greasy jaws. Only Cap stood off a ways, giving me a look I couldn't figure but took as a warning, and so for the rest of that day, while I went west towards the Rio Grande, I kept making switchbacks and waiting when I made one to see if I was being followed, but I wasn't, and after a few days of this I fetched up at a tiny Mex village called Questa where I worked for a man who needed help getting in his second cutting of hay.

When the crop was laid by I went down to Taos, where the whiskey comes from and, so they say, used to be a popular gathering spot for trappers and hunters where they drank and threw knives, and made use of the gals from an Indian village nearby. All that kind of stuff was long gone when I got there: no hairy fellers out of the mountains, no Indian gals I could find on the loose. Whorehouses, yes, which I visited, and the whiskey that, now that I was next to a plentiful supply, I found myself dipping into pretty regular. For work, I found it in a café on the plaza where I cut up potatoes, onions, peppers, and the like, swept floors, wiped off tables, and washed dishes. This was the first indoors job I ever had—and almost the last. I had worked for other men before, but not like this, where you was obliged to take orders all day and into the night—bring me this, and be quick about it—from customers wasn't no better than you, if they was as good, but acted like they was king of the castle. I found it didn't suit me. Even working for Kip Brown, you was in a manner of speaking still your own man a good deal of the time, off by yourself minding the edges of the herd, being on night guard with only the coyotes and sleepy cattle for company. Hard work, sure, but not as hard on me as the café.

A thing happened there however that quick made me glad enough to be where I'd landed. One day a man rode into the plaza with two horses behind him packing dead men. Of course, we all turned out to see the new show come to town, and if that kind of thing interests you, it was worth your while to get in line to see what had been drug in. The bodies was bad beat up, having been some days on the trail through rough country, as ugly to look at as Tunstall when they brought him down past my place. Here, it turned out they was wanted men a bounty hunter was bringing in to collect his reward money. When I was able to inspect them up close, I was pretty certain one of them come from that filthy nest up near the Red. That sent me back to my chores with a lighter step. But this didn't last long, and just when I was about over it the news come that Garrett had killed the Kid at Fort Sumner.

*

Of course, it being the Kid there had to be a whole herd of rumors that come along with his death. A few made you think, but most was just foolishness. The one you heard most was that Garrett shot the wrong man but then quick covered up his mistake in a new-dug grave: a man had him surprised in the dark of Pete Maxwell's bedroom and Garrett had shot blind, so to say. Then, when they brung in a lantern, they seen it wasn't the Kid at all and just dumped the unlucky feller in a grave next to Bowdre and Tom O'Folliard. The other popular one was just about the same, except that here they had Garrett knowing goddamn well it wasn't the Kid but shot anyways, figuring a dead stiff underground might be as good as a famous outlaw.

Both of these have to be wrong, if you think about it a bit. In order for either one to be the case, Garrett would have to do a hell of a lot of fixing up to bring them off, and do it right quick, too. He would have to get Pete Maxwell to go along with the trick and at the same time Paulita Maxwell, who was there soon as the shots was heard; also, his deputies, Poe and Tip McKinney. This ain't very likely. And this ain't the half of it. There was also the neighbors that all knew the Kid and quick gathered around and seen the body. Some of them made remarks ugly enough to cause Garrett and his deputies to spend the rest of that night there in Maxwell's bedroom with their guns drawn. Till the day he got bushwhacked himself, Garrett had sworn enemies over in what's now De Baca County: you ain't a sworn enemy, pardner, over a strange stiff. They knew who Garrett had killed, all right, and, like I earlier said, some yet believe Garrett was killed by someone avenging the Kid.

One other story you heard was never as popular as the wrong-man ones, yet you'd hear it now and again: it was said that Pete Maxwell was sore at the Kid for taking advantage of his little sister, and so when Garrett asked him about the Kid just when the Kid was backing into the room, Maxwell said, 'That's him, right there!' Everbody around Sumner knew about Paulita and the Kid. Soon as Wally Burns got down that way, writing on his book, he heard about them and actually asked Paulita about it. She said it weren't so. But what Burns couldn't ask was another part of that story and a mighty big part: when Garrett killed the Kid, Paulita was carrying the Kid's baby.

Not that long after the Kid was killed, Paulita married a feller named Jaramillo, and not too long after that she had a baby boy. Could have been his, of course—Jaramillo's, I mean. Such things was not unknown then, though hardly common. Cella's sister had a girl some months after marrying, and while I never inquired about just how many months that was, I have the notion it wasn't no nine. There's people yet around Roswell that'll tell you Paulita's boy by Billy grew up and lives there yet. Looks a good deal like his daddy, they say. I never seen him, but it's queer to think there could be a feller with rabbit teeth and them cold eyes, running around loose.

Well, this here's what I heard from Garrett, right outside my gate when he left here that morning after our two days together—

last time I ever saw him. I had fed him breakfast, and he thanked me for it, kind of brisk-like, and went out to his horse. When he had saddled up, I went to open the gate, and he come past with his hat kind of slouched down over his eyes and not looking at me, as if he'd had all the palaver he wanted with George Coe. But goddamn, if I didn't find myself asking him another question when he turned down the path to the river. Then I hollered at him, '*Ain't you going to tell me how it happened?!*'

Soon as it was out of my mouth I knew how terrible unmannerly it was—me, hollering that at *Pat Garrett!* By Godfrey, a man, especially *that* man, has got to be entitled to his secrets and not have to be hounded by ever jackass that wants to bust into his privacy just to satisfy some foolish curiosity. But, hell, he'd already given me just about everthing else on the subject, why leave the ending off? You see here how my thinking was going—not anything I was proud of at the time, nor for some time after. Now, so many years has come between, the shame's kind of faded from me. Practically everbody connected to the matter is dead, while I'm still living along and seem to have come to easier terms with what I done.

He knew right well what 'it' meant. Had to. He'd been carrying 'it' around with him all them years and knowing that whatever man he happened to be talking with, wherever, on whatever subject—water, politics, horses—was just itching to pry inside him, so to put it, and find out how it was when he killed the Kid.

He reined in but didn't turn around in the saddle, just turned his head partway in my direction and started talking, low-like. 'I was sitting on Maxwell's bed trying to get information, which was hard: he was sleeping off a drunk and wasn't making good sense. A man come in on me, real quiet, and it was so dark I couldn't much make him out. But when he talked low to Pete,— "Who are them hombres outside"—I knew the voice and pulled and fired all in one motion. Then I run outside with Pete right on my tail. Poe and McKinney had seen the Kid on his way into the house but hadn't recognized him and thought I had shot the wrong man. Pete didn't know what to think but got a lantern and leaned it in through the window. There he was on his back with his eyes open—you could see the lantern light in them. I got him dead center.'

He faced back around then and clucked to his horse. Going away, he said something that sounded like 'Luck.' And you maybe know how it is: if you tell yourself some story enough times, what you *think* you heard comes to be what you *know* you heard, for certain. Who can say what he meant? Maybe he was saying his shot in the dark was lucky. Or maybe he was only wishing me luck.

X

Not that long after the news about the Kid, I got disgusted with the café. When I think back now on my days in Taos and the death of the Kid, it's clear to me that I had come to the end of one part of my life. But at the time, all I knew was that I didn't want to work in the café no more. So, I just went across the plaza to work as a barkeep—not much of a change, you'll say. But it was movement along a path, though I didn't stay long there, neither: I quick enough got crosswise with a customer and reached over and conked him on his big ugly skull with a bottle. Fortunately for the both of us the bottle was heavy enough so it didn't break and cut his head off, or else I might have been hung for murder. I quit before the owner could fire me, and shortly thereafter Mud and me was on the trail south out of town to Ranchos, then east, then south some more. If I was to say to you I was headed somewheres, that would be a lie. I wasn't going nowhere in particular but had become once again one of them drifters I spoke of before, the kind that seems drawn to any big, open territory that don't have any shape to it yet but is only a empty space on the map, with here and there a dot that stands for a spot where there's water enough to slap up some buildings. Seems like it's just the emptiness of such places that's the draw for such fellers, like just maybe they got some sort of new chances there that they didn't have previous in more settled spots. Or maybe it's that they want to get away from whatever was making them unhappy, and so they just keep a-going and a-going. That description would fit me at the time I'm telling of, but, like I say, at least I was moving.

I hadn't got very far along this southward trail when I come upon a feller that had turned aside into a small meadow where he was tending to his horse. Turned out it had a problem with a frog, and the feller asked me did I have a thin blade he could use to prize out whatever might be caught in there; what he had on him was about the size of a cavalry sword, and he could hardly work fine with it. Also, he wondered if I might have some of that salve made out of tree sap that was commonly used for that condition. I had me the one but not the other, and so together—him steadying the horse and me working the pick—we tried to remove the problem but couldn't spot nothing. The frog looked oozy enough, all right, but we couldn't find why. Whatever, it did appear to me the feller hadn't been too careful with the horse right along. Finally, I said we might try to make up a kind of poultice out of bacon grease and a plant that grows along high-country creek beds that is strong enough to draw out whatever don't belong in that soft part of the hoof, something I learned from Doc Scurlock when we was out on the trail during the war. There was a bit of a creek on the far side of the meadow—more like a seep—, but I couldn't find nothing that looked like what Doc had used, and so what we ended up trying was the bacon grease, a good bunch of meadow grass, and a piece of the feller's long johns tied around the fetlock to keep everthing in place. That, I said, and a few days' rest might turn the trick. The feller said he wasn't in no hurry to arrive any-wheres, and, as it was by that point coming on towards sundown, we concluded to camp where we was and share what we had.

Name was Bloodworth Jones, a name that would stick with you, and he said he was from Texas but had been long gone from there. Like many back then he'd spent some years on the south-ern buffalo range and then went up into Colorado and Wyoming, following where it was said the herds had moved to get away from

160

the hunters. There had once been so many buff nobody could believe they was hunted out, not even the Indians, who you would think would have known best. He was a red-haired feller with a bit of beard that was patchy enough to make you think he weren't growing it on purpose. Humorous devil, always looking to find the fun in something, no matter what: here he was, in the middle of nowhere with a lame horse, talking with a perfect stranger in the night, and nobody waiting for him at the end of his trail, just laughing the night along. He had been drifting like this for some years and had got as far west as Arizona, which he found didn't suit him at all—said it was so dry it hurt to fart. Now he was thinking about going back to Texas, but didn't seem to be making much progress in that direction, having been moving northward through New Mexico until he got sidetracked by a gal in Trampas that had given him a proper dose. Said he believed he might have give it to his horse, causing it to go lame, same as him. I asked about that town, and he told me it wasn't much of a place, and what there was was strange on account of some sort of secret society they had there where the members whipped one another with cactus ropes till they was bloody. Still and all, he thought he might have been there yet, only the gal's father, who was the big chief of the secret society, caught him trying to spy on them and run him out of town.

Like I said, Bloodworth was a humorous character, and I didn't know just how much of his foolery was the truth, but as I was already headed in that general direction, I figured I might as well continue on and have a look for myself: it ain't ever day you get a chance to see white men acting like savages. So the next morning I left Bloodworth and his lame horse behind and took the trail towards Trampas, which went up and up, through aspen and spruce and ponderosa, but I wasn't on no lame horse, as Mud hadn't been doing a thing in Taos except get fat and sleek, and now he relished the work. We kept on that way till well into the afternoon when up ahead I heard noises, and Mud flicked his ears. I reined in and listened, and after a bit there come the noises again. Somewheres ahead there was a man talking high and yelling ever once in a while, so I went on careful to a place where there was a kind of nest of boulders with some ponderosas around it, as good a place as you could want to have a look at what you might be riding into. While I was tying Mud to a branch and snaking out my rifle I was wondering if Bloodworth might have been telling the truth and that this commotion was a meeting of that secret society where they was using whips on one another. But no.

What it was was old Galvez down in a little dell-like place where he was being held up by a big, dark-looking hombre that kept waving his pistol at him while he picked through the packets he had pulled off Galvez's mule. This was making him mad enough to holler, as he couldn't find nothing valuable in his plunder, and while I watched he begun kicking things about and waving that pistol in Galvez's face, such that things was looking very ugly. I drew a bead on the robber's back, ready to squeeze off a shot, but just then that queer feeling come over me again, where I knew this was a moment I was bound to remember the rest of my days, just like at Blazer's Mill.

It wasn't the condition itself: I had aimed at a man and shot him, too, so I was familiar with what it took, and this here was a well-nigh perfect setup. My rifle was resting in a notch between the boulders and I had a clear view sixty yards downslope at that feller threatening old Galvez, a man I had some feeling for, even if I didn't know why. I knew I couldn't miss, everthing being so sharp and clear. But then this feeling was sharp and clear as well: did I really want to kill this fucker, snuff his lamp, just like that? Did I want to cripple him up so he had to drag himself through life in terrible pain? Or was I positioned up here to *save* a life— old Galvez's, I mean—instead of taking one? And was it really me, George Coe, thinking like this, or was it something coming off Galvez, like smoke drifting up towards me?

I have since come to know this much, anyways, about that moment: you ain't ever going to be able to explain such a thing to another person, and as soon as you try for that, you can hear how it ain't coming out right and so has no chance of ending up right, neither. It's like me trying to tell you what it felt like looking into the Kid's eyes or Garrett trying to say how it felt to kill him. Here, in this thing, I once tried telling Cella, but at that time I was already having plenty of trouble courting her on account of my dangerous past without her coming to believe I was also loco, so I quit. But she had already heard enough to ask, 'Did you kill the robber?' And I said I hadn't, which was God's truth. What I done instead was to shoot behind him, and both him and Galvez jumped a mile. Then I quick shot to one side of him and the other, so he knew he was boxed in by somebody firing from good cover. All this while Galvez was shouting, but I was too busy to hear him—'Don't kill him!' 'Don't kill him!' Finally, I did hear and hollered down to the feller to throw his pistol away from him to where I could see it good, which he done. Then I come down into the dell with another slug chambered in.

Up close, he was one mean-looking son of a bitch and a good half again my size. But like Colonel Colt says, a gun is a mighty good equalizer and never more so than when one feller has throwed his away, while you still got yours. I could've been a dwarf or some such, and still I would have had him, and I could see that in his face: he was a scared badman, all right. Behind him there was Galvez, standing still and watchful but his eyes steady and looking just like he had when I first met him. He had jumped high at my first shot, but he had come back down, whereas the big robber was still way up in the air, so to put it. He stayed that way while I picked up his pistol, which didn't look that reliable with its loose hammer, and then I went through his saddlebags for further weapons: he had a seven-shot Spencer, but it didn't look that much better than the sidearm and made me wonder whether this feller didn't *beat* his victims out of their money instead of shooting them. I told him to get his dirty ass out of there quick before I put another hole in it. For all the hollering he done that had brung him to my attention in the first place he become a mighty quiet man—never said one word this entire time—and rode off that same way, never once looking back.

'If he can lay hands on a weapon somewheres,' I told old Galvez, 'he'll likely come back and dry-gulch the both of us. We had best move along quick, so let's gather up your things, and I'll ride along with you to wherever you're headed.'

'"The man that stayeth his hand in battle is blessed of the Lord,"' he said. 'I am going to Las Trampas.' Much later on I asked him about what he had quoted out of the Bible, and he said it was from Proverbs, but I never found it there. Anyways, we begun gathering his things, which was flang here and there, the same bundles I had seen back at La Cueva. Some was busted open and others just dropped where they was, and Galvez done most of the gathering, as he knew what went where, whereas I didn't know what most of the stuff was and would stand there stupid, staring at what I was holding until Galvez come along and took it to its proper place. All this while I was in something of a hurry, thinking about that big robber with murder in his eyes, but not Galvez: he went about things, slow and careful, replacing everthing just so until he was done and satisfied, the last item being that thing I had took for a ladder back at La Cueva. Now he said it was an easel that you put your painting on.

Of course, I knew well enough what an artist was, and like everbody else I had seen pictures on the wall—ever saloon them days had a picture up above the bar, usually a naked lady or a Indian or a buffalo, though never all together. Yet somehow, I hadn't ever had occasion to connect in my mind a picture with the man who done it and still less with just *how* he done it. It was kind of like the old saying about a fire: you could look at a picture of one with the flames and all; you could sit by one somebody else had made for you; but you wouldn't truly know what a fire was until you had gathered the wood for it and built it and then used it to cook a meal on. Then, by Godfrey, you got it. This ain't to say that I got it about Galvez's materials and how they was used, but it begun there when I helped him put them on the mule and we rode on towards Trampas.

*

Bloodworth spoke the truth about Trampas, all right. It sure as hell didn't look like much. There was a wall all the way around it, but it was more holes than wall. Houses was small, and the ones I seen looked to be but one room wide, though some was fairly long. The only thing that had something to it was the church, which was thick-built and had matching wooden towers. Them shabby little houses grouped around it looked almost like they was praying to it, and maybe that was the idea.

Now, I had been in Mexican villages before—lots—, and had spent some weeks in San Patricio, as I mentioned, but this here was a different deal. Compared to Trampas, San Patricio looked new, where Trampas looked like it had been put up by the *ancestors* of the Mexicans, them that was said to have come through here years and years before Santa Ana, wearing iron helmets that must've cooked their brains like porridge in a skillet. Everthing here looked ancient, including the folks that come out to greet Galvez and guide him along. Even the young ones looked old, old and dark, where the folks at San Patricio was mostly a lightish brown. But yet, in amongst all of them, Galvez looked the most ancient, like he was *their* ancestor and had worn one of them helmets and rode a mustang instead of a mule. This thought come to me while I went along behind him, but it come back to me even stronger that night when I had bedded down in a lean-to outside the house where Galvez was guest of honor. It was black as mud in there; I couldn't see no stars or nothing, and as I laid there in the straw I was thinking that my wanderings away from my kin on the Sugarite had landed me in a spot that didn't seem to have no time to it at all and where the people whipped one another bloody since they didn't have nothing else to do.

I may say here that I wasn't raised up to have thoughts about ghostly things; Frank neither, though it's true that some nights back in Missouri when we was sharing a bed we'd talk that way—spooking each other with talk of goblins and such, as kids will do. But the grownups around us was just down-to-earth sorts, and we never heard talk of unearthly things like goblins nor ghosts. What you heard talk of was weather, crops, prices, livestock, and fencing. Far as that goes, I don't believe I was ever in a church as a kid, where naturally you might hear such talk. Maybe it would have been different if my mother had lived and I had been raised in one place; she might have seen to my religion, and told me about the Holy Ghost and such things. But here I was in a black lean-to in a village built around a church and where it looked like nobody from the rest of the world had been in here in ages, maybe since forever. And the only soul I knew was a feller who might be like a ghost himself, hundreds and hundreds of years old, like the men in the Bible.

All this, pardner, made for a peculiar night, and the next morning after the roosters and dogs had come on duty I felt like I had been whipped hard myself through the night and put up bloody. But when I dragged myself out into the daylight, there was old Galvez, smoking and talking friendly with the man of the house, and everthing looked so daily, so to say, that I felt shameful and so crawled back into the lean-to for my sack of makings and then joined them for a smoke in the sun, which sure felt good.

Vigil—that was the man's name that owned the house—was a woodworker, and he put the busted easel back together, explaining as he went along what hadn't been done proper in the first place by a woodworker from another village. (Later, Galvez told me he had a good opinion of that other feller and was glad to have the work of both on the easel.) Then me and Galvez went to work, going over to the church which sat close to the wall, me carrying the easel with its bright new wood and various packets of the materials that Galvez had pointed out. Vigil's little boy come along with a three-legged stool, the two of us marching along behind Galvez, like we was his soldiers. It's true, he moved fairly slow, but there wasn't none of that pausing-along and head-cocking and measuring-out with your thumb like you will sometimes see with these shit-ass painters that show up nowadays at the county fair with a big hat and a long, pointy beard and have a pile of pictures where their name is wrote as big as whatever it is they want you to buy. No, sir, Galvez knew just where he was headed and wasn't taking no measurements: it was plain he was familiar with ever part of that church and had painted it many a time before. So, when we got to the right spot, he had the kid set the stool down just so while I put up the easel and set the materials down careful: little bottles of water, ox gall, paint boxes, tiny sponges, cloths, pencils with big leads, all the stuff that today you can buy in a store—and even back then Galvez bought some of his equipment when he went to Santa Fe. But most was hand-made, from the cakes of paint to the brushes (which was made of squirrel fur) to the ox gall, which he got in the villages where he stopped. Even what's called the ferrule was handmade by a tinsmith in Cordova. But however you come by your materials, it's the hand that makes the difference. Anybody can get hold of a .41 Thunderer—nice compact sidearm that handles easy with almost no kick—but few can use it like the Kid. None, maybe.

Same with Galvez and his brushes. I have been around a few artists when they was at work, but I never seen one to match old Galvez once he put the brush to the paper, and down to this very moment I have a picture of him in my mind, just as he was that morning behind San José de Gracia church with the big slant of the shadow coming down from one of the towers, and him looking hard at it for a moment, then starting at the top of his sheet: big, thick black line, raking along so you could hear the brush going against the paper's grain if you was close enough, and the whole outline taking shape out of nothing, so to say. And so here again, that ghostly feeling come over me, and I was thinking, 'Who in hell *is* this feller, anyways?!' And him paying nobody any mind, looking steady at the church but never down at his work, which, by Godfrey, seemed to be doing itself, like as if his hand was being pulled along by something else. Meanwhile, the Vigil kid was looking on same as me and some other little ones come over as well. By midpoint in the afternoon a fair number had come and gone, along with the village's dogs that was looking for scraps, but there wasn't none as Galvez never ate and only took a few sips of water out of an old army canteen. By then he'd finished with his outlines and was working with his other paints, putting in his colors and then rubbing some of this out and working on other spaces with the heavy-leaded pencils. Then, after some hours at this, he laid the brushes and pencils down careful on the lip of the easel and said the light had now changed too much, and he was done for the day. So, we packed up and moved along to another house where we was to spend the night, though this time I didn't get a lean-to, as the family had a full mess of kids that took up ever bit of space: I slept out with Mud and Año-Año, the mule, but this wasn't no hardship, as I had done so many a time before and liked it better than the lean-to, which felt a tad too coffin-like for my taste. A man who stopped once to buy my pictures told me there are monks over in Spain that sleep in the coffins they'll be buried in. If that's so, it seems to me like rushing things a tad, don't you think?

Next morning, same thing: smoke, coffee, flour tortilla with Mex sausage, and then to work at the same spot where that afternoon Galvez finished the painting. In the evening after supper he took it back to Vigil's and give it to him. Next day he begun yet another, this one from several feet further on, towards the back of the church. So it went, with him working along, a few feet at a time, around the back and then up the other side, and the paintings kept on coming.

I believe we might have been in Trampas a little more than a week, with Galvez giving away each painting to the family we had stayed with. All of them folks was friendly as you could want, though there wasn't no back-slapping or none of that where Galvez was concerned: they was very careful of him and let him have his distance in the house and at the table. Food was plentiful enough but rough on a white man's bowels on account of they had lots of them peppers they favor in everthing except tortillas. Maybe, if there had been some whiskey available, I might have had a better time with it, but there wasn't. There was one feller had a big jug of tequila, which always smelled to me like puke when you went to have your first drink, but even at that, I thought it was better than nothing. When Galvez told me one day it was time we moved along to Truchas I was hopeful the food might improve there, but it didn't. I never have gotten used to the way Mexes cook.

*

At Truchas the routine was the same: Galvez painted the church from different angles and give the paintings to the families we stayed with. Same in Cordova, where we went next and where we put up with two woodworkers; one of them had built the easel the big robber kicked to pieces. But as I tell you all this, you'll notice I ain't telling nothing about what went on between me and Galvez, on account of there ain't nothing to tell. I did what he told me he wanted done, and by the time we fetched up in Cordova, I could pretty well figure out what that was going to be. He was a man of very few words, and now that I was onto his daily routine we hardly spoke at all. Around the villagers I noticed him somewhat more talkative, but not that much, and as it was always in Mexican I never understood any of it. Maybe if I had, some of the things I was puzzling over wouldn't have appeared as mysterious as they did.

Looking back on them first weeks, it's clear enough now that Galvez was sizing me up to see if I might do as a hand. He needed someone, as I seen from our first meeting, where I helped him up on Año-Año at La Cueva. So, along with packing and unpacking his gear, setting up the easel, and so forth, I also seen to that animal, who wasn't the easiest critter to be around. Later on, when I had sort of proved myself, he trusted me with other chores, especially reshaping his brushes with water when his day's work was done, and this come as an honor, on account of you have to know what a brush is supposed to look like before you go to reshaping it. I made my mistakes at first, of course, but I had been looking sharp at them brushes right along, and fairly soon he made it plain to me that he was satisfied with my work, only once in a while taking a brush from me and showing me what it ought to look like.

But a good hand ain't only being useful with chores; it's also disposition, especially if you're out working with your boss, just the two of you. If you're the jabbering sort who ain't comfortable without some chin music always going on, and your boss ain't built that way, you ain't the right man for him, and sooner or later he'll let you know that. Here on my place I've had a man or two I had to let go for that reason. Even if Bloodworth Jones had been a top hand—which I don't believe he ever was—, he wouldn't have stuck long with old Galvez. As it was, since the war I had become a solitary sort, not much given to talk, even when having a drink, and this turned out to be just right for Galvez, who I gradually learned had been moving slowly along trails to these villages for many years, just him and the mules he rode till they wore out. But if he'd come across me in my earlier days—

say, when I was helling about up at them hog ranches—, why, he wouldn't have stood for me past our first night in Trampas.

When I look at it like this, as I have done over time, I see now that all the misfortunes I had been feeling so sore about wasn't misfortunes after all, as they was the very things that made me fit in with Galvez's requirements. And I'm including even having this here finger shot off and then shooting that feller during the big shootout and crippling him and maybe finally killing him, too. What I mean by this is that when I heard the big robber hollering through the trees, all them things I had gone through in the war was inside me, way down in there, and so when I drew that bead on him, I was a different feller at that particular moment than I had been before and was able to have the thoughts that suddenly come over me behind them boulders. Probably saved Galvez's life there—probably saved the robber's as well, though I think it likely he went on to do more robberies, till somebody else had to kill him.

I probably saved my own life, too, but I didn't know none of this then, nor even well after I commenced riding with Galvez. This was quite a while coming to me, and I had to earn my spurs, as they say, all the way to when my days with Galvez was coming to a close, him having got so feeble I had to lift him in my arms to get him into the saddle, and then had to ride mighty close to him holding a leather strap that went around his waist so he didn't fall off—which one day he finally did. But down through all them years, from the time I didn't dust the big robber, I was puzzling and puzzling over that special moment, until one day I tied it to a scripture Galvez quoted more regular than any other: 'Whosoever will save his life shall lose it. And whosoever will lose his life for my sake shall find it.' You can look it up; it's in Matthew.

*

The beginning of the end for us come in a place on the Mora called Golondrinas. I've been back to it many a time since, as it has a special meaning to me and have done my own painting of the church, though it ain't up to Galvez's.

It was spring, and a rainy one, which is good for crops, but not so good if you're trying to paint outside. This day begun sunny, though, and the whole village was out in the fields, fixing up the ditches, including the women with food and water and their kids alongside. Galvez and me was over at the church, but when we had set out he said he wasn't feeling his best, and I could see that was so, as that dark hacked wood he had for a face looked liverish. Still, we set up across the road where you looked up at the church, which had the usual flock of swallows darting around it, and he went back to work on a painting he'd started some days previous but had put aside while waiting for a turn in the weather. You could tell, though, by the way he handled himself that he was off his feed: fidgeting around on the stool, hesitating with his hand, drawing it back: quite unlike him while at work. Finally, he sets the brush down and says he wasn't working well and wanted to lie down, a thing he had never said in all our years together. The place we was staying was at the upper edge of the village, and while Golondrinas weren't a large place, it was a bit of a walk upslope to the house, and when we started I seen right off he wasn't going to make it, so I steered him into the church and a bench where he laid down. Then I went back for the canteen.

While I was at this a big cloud come over the sun. There wasn't much light in the church anyways, and it was dim enough when I got back inside it that when I spotted him, I quick thought he was dead: just laying there with his mouth open and them great big hands folded on his chest like you see when a man's been laid out by the undertaker. When I bent over him, though, I seen his chest rising and falling, slow and steady under his hands, and so my own chest commenced to slow down some. I sat down on the next bench and waited, wondering what I was meant to do, and it was a fair spell before he opened his eyes at last and looked straight up at the vigas, staring hard at 'em, and not looking nowheres else. Maybe he was thinking he'd died and here was heaven—natural enough for a man in his line of work—, but then his eyes commenced traveling about some and come at last to rest on me, which sure as hell would have told him he was yet on earth. Still, it didn't seem somehow that he knew just where he was. And maybe I've said enough already for you to imagine how this might have struck me, as over time I had been relying on him to know almost everthing needful, from what we was going to do next, to the right trail to take, to where the littlest brush was in his quiver.

'Sixty years,' he suddenly come out, 'sixty years'—I ain't going to try talking like him, just give the words and not how they sounded. 'Sixty years I have been on the trail to here.' So, here again, I figured he must think he's dying. And maybe there was something like that in his thoughts, because what come out then in a long rope of talking was all about himself and the life he'd lived that in some way had begun right here in Golondrinas and had come back here again, maybe for good. In all the years we had been on the trail together I never had heard him say one word about himself. *Nothing.* If a man don't ever tell you anything about his past, you're apt to figure he's got something back there he don't care to mention, something he's hiding: common enough back then. But with Galvez, somehow it didn't feel like that to me. It was more like he wasn't put together like the rest of us, that he didn't have an age to him, the years that made up a past. But now, here the past come. I don't want to look at it like it was a confession; it was more like him saying out loud what it was like being him, take it or leave it.

At first, his voice was a bit quavery, so I had to lean close to get what he was saying, but as he went on it become strong and determined-sounding. He was from just over the Colorado border near what's now a good-sized town, Durango, but way back whenever this was, it must have been a small place like the ones we customarily stopped at in New Mexico. The family had some sort of spread, maybe sizeable, as there was many mouths to feed: eight children, then three more that come to them when an aunt moved in after the Cheyennes killed her husband.

Some time after this—Galvez didn't say the years—there come a morning when three mares was missing, and Galvez's father said a troublesome buckskin stud had run them off, not the first time this had happened. His pa give Galvez a rifle and a horse and told him to find the bunch and bring them back, and if the buckskin give any trouble, to shoot him, as he weren't worth the continued aggravation.

The trail away from the spread was plain, and once on it Galvez knew where it was going, and, sure enough, when he had got on the other side of a stand of woods there was a box canyon and a meadow with good grass and water and the buckskin was there with the three mares: he was fixing to set up housekeeping on his own and not have to bother with competition from other studs, nor human interference. Galvez figured on some trouble but was on a good horse that kept the stud in the box until the mares was lined up and headed back homeward with the buckskin running along with them. When they got into the woods again, all of a sudden the mares spooked and wheeled back and the buckskin, too, and while Galvez was fighting to get his horse back under control he seen a flash of something ahead. It was another horse, loose in the trees and saddled but riderless. He recognized the horse, had ridden it himself, but what in Sam Hill was it doing out here? He sat there a moment, not knowing what his next move should be, with the mares and the stud running back toward the box canyon, the loose horse going the other way, and the missing rider somewhere in between and surely in some kind of trouble. He let the mares and the stud go back the way they come, figuring he could collect them again, and instead picked his way up towards where he'd first seen the horse. He hadn't got far when he heard the whicker of still another horse, which his own horse answered. Then old Galvez stopped talking, and I seen tears running down them deep cracks in his face. So then, I myself was kind of like the young Galvez of his story, not knowing what to do or say. Had to sit there and wait for him to go on, just like the young Galvez moving slow uphill towards the other horse.

'I come upon them,' he says finally, still looking up at the vigas. It was an older brother, Tomás, and one of the girls that had come into the family after the Cheyennes killed her father up in Colorado. They was both trying to get their clothes back on but hadn't yet. 'I shot Tomás where he stood,' Galvez said. 'I slew my brother in the field, like Cain. And then I rode away and never come back to my family. I was Cain, but without a mark that would tell others to take pity on me.'

*

You won't have no trouble, I expect, understanding how this story made me feel. I was a wanted man, too, and maybe a killer, to boot, though it's true I hadn't killed my blood brother—a big difference. But in other ways as well I was like Galvez, had been since the end of the war, drifting here and there, looking for something, I didn't know what; or maybe for somebody to take pity on me, until I come upon an old man, trying to get back up on his mule and took pity on him. But the real thing here, the truth, was that Galvez took pity on *me* by letting me come along with him, village after village, until we come to Golondrinas, where he appeared to believe he was dying or maybe even dead, and so at last said out loud what the trail had been like all them years: one place and then another; one kind of work and then another—farm hand, miner, blacksmith, which is what he was when he'd first fetched up in Golondrinas. But here, so it had turned out, what they needed at that particular moment more than a blacksmith was a man to put a coat of paint on the doors and window frames of their church, which was new, and he told them he could do it.

He said the first time he took hold of the brush and begun applying the paint, it was like something was traveling from the brush to his hand, then up his arm and into his chest and then down here, below his belly, and he just *knew* how the paint was to go on, the thickness, how to turn the brush into the corners without splattering it on the walls, how to hold the brush when working high above your head and when you're coming down below your waist, but not quite at that point where you can get down on your knees. After he had finished, the folks was pleased enough to where a man asked him to paint his front door and a fence, and then another the same. Didn't pay nothing, only a place out of the weather, plus his meals. But he found that he could live (which is maybe not quite the same as making a living, if by that you mean making a profit) as a painter of sorts. Then there come a day in Dalia where, when he had finished his work on the church—was working inside by now, doing close-up painting around the altar—, he found a long scrap of rough paper that had print on one side, but the back was empty. And he took the small brush he'd been using and drew the outline of the altar.

That was the start of it all, him going along, blacksmithing still, but more and more painting and some plastering, too, which he said taught him some things about thickness, and so forth. Wherever he was, he always made time to do little paintings of the churches. They was mighty poor, he said, but slowly got to look more like what he was aiming at. At Gavilan he fell in with a sure-enough painter named Tito and learned some tricks from him and ended up shoeing Tito's horse in trade for two fine-pointed brushes. Some years thereafter, him and Tito's paths crossed again in Truchas, where Tito was living with two brothers and their families.

The brothers was what they called *hermanos*, which is brothers in Mexican. But these was not just brothers in the flesh; they was also brothers in blood, so they believed, and in the spirit. Turns out they was part of that very same bunch Bloodworth had mentioned to me as the cause of him having to hightail it out of Trampas, runny pecker, lame horse, and all. These *hermanos* was actually located in a good many of them little villages in the north country, and what they was was a religious outfit that tries to help out their neighbors in times of need. They believe they are all sinners in God's eyes, and so do good works to make up for it, that and whip themselves and carry great, heavy crosses, penalty-like. One time when I was with old Galvez, we was in El Porvenir, and he said he had something else to attend to, and as I was bored with the village on that particular day with nothing to do, I took Rooster—that was my horse after Mud—and rode east of town a fair ways when it commenced raining real hard. I was too far out to easily turn back into town and was looking about for any barn or shed or lean-to for shelter when I seen an odd-looking building and made for it. It was half underground, so a man on horseback could pret' near touch the rooftop, and had but two small windows. I could see the hasp on the door didn't have no lock to it, so I tied Rooster under a clump of piñons and then run around and got inside, soaked through at that point.

It was a kind of church but had only seats for maybe half a dozen people and an altar that was back in like a little cave with a fence in front and a opening where you could go up to the altar, if you had business up there. Over in a corner off the altar was a stack of five or six long wood crosses, and, pardner, if those was what was carried by the *hermanos*, they was some mighty heavy sins they was trying to work off. No wonder Galvez fell in with them, which is what he said happened with him—him carrying around the killing of Tomás. And that weren't even all of his load, bad as it was. Turned out that Galvez himself had had his eyes on that very same gal as Tomás, and had gone so far as to begin scheming in his mind for a way he might get off somewheres with her. 'I killed Tomás for his sin,' he said to the ceiling, 'but more for the sin I wished to commit but had not yet.' Ain't *that* something, though, to carry along in your saddlebags!? So the whipping and the carrying of them great, heavy crosses, and I don't know what else—that was just what he'd been looking for but hadn't known till he fell in with it.

How long he was a brother or if maybe he still was, I can't say. But what he did say to the ceiling was that somewheres along the way he come to understand that good works can come in all different shapes, and that he had been given the gift of being able to paint pictures of churches for a reason. And the reason was so that after some years ever man in each village would have a painting up on his wall that would be a reminder of what was owed God and that they was all God's children, and was bound to treat everbody according to that condition. That was what he meant when he said his long trail had led him back to this place where it all begun and where he was painting the church again to give it to another man to put up on his wall and look at it ever morning, sun or rain or Sunday.

"'Whosoever will save his life shall lose it,'" he says, looking at me for the first time since he begun talking. That had been quite a spell, and I could tell by how dark it had got inside the church that it was coming on toward sundown. "'And whosoever will lose his life for my sake shall find it.'" Then he says for me to help him to his feet, and we went out of the church and up towards where we was staying, meeting along our way the first of the women coming home from the fields.

178

XI

H e weren't ever the same after Golondrinas. Nothing was said; we just went about our business through summer but with him ever more feeble, like I said, and not firm with the brush in hand. His outlines, which was always so black and heavy now looked like what a spider might make if it had ink on its legs. At the end of the summer, when the days begun to get a snap to them and there was flakes of snow at night, our custom was to begin to move down from the high country, through Holman and Buena Vista, Sapello, and like that, making for Cañoncito, which was our last stop before Santa Fe, and this is what we done now, but slower still. (Somewhere around here, or maybe down to the river house, I got a honey of a painting of the little church there, Nuestra Señora de la Luz; remind me to show it to you before you leave.) At Cañoncito he only done one painting and that one not finished, and then we left for Santa Fe where Galvez liked to put up for the winter. We had been on the trail a couple of hours when he just sort of . . . quit.

Bright, sunny day, more like September than late November, and we was taking it careful, and then it was like everthing just stopped for him, and he slumped sideways toward me. Before I could haul in line and catch him he went under my horse, which stepped on him. He made a small sound like, '*Ohh,*' and I was able to get the horse aside without further damage. There we was, maybe five miles from town and the day the short kind that come with that season. Other than to turn him over and put blankets over him and under his head I couldn't do nothing for him, and his face was almost white and teeth hard clenched so that when I tried to give him water, the canteen clattered against 'em. All this while he was staring at me *fierce*, like he was trying to tell me something important, but damn if I could figure what it might be. I talked to him a bit and said several times that I wasn't going to leave him, that I would stay with him till help come. Must have been over an hour when help did come along: two wagons of woodcutters, hauling from Rowe to town, and one of them knew Galvez. They shifted their loads to make room for him in one of the wagons, and we fit him in there with me sitting atop a woodpile, trying to steady him against the way the road went.

*

Our destination was the home of a feller named Antonio Vigil who was related to the Vigil in Trampas and lived over on Galisteo Street in what used to be a dance hall. Galvez always liked the setup there, watching winter come on, repairing his materials, adding new ones in trade, and resting up. On fine days such as can come to Santa Fe in the midst of January, he might take a walk down to the plaza and be gone three hours or more, but that was about it. Rest of the time he pretty much stayed put, though always busy at something. I stayed out back in a casita, sharing a part of it with Rooster and the mule.

When we got there with the wagons Vigil quick sent for the doc, who said Galvez had broke his shoulder, but that what caused the fall was some kind of heart failure. When he finished, he took Vigil aside and said he judged the old man's trail-riding days was done, that it would be dangerous for him to continue. I heard that, same as Vigil, and both of us knew that if Galvez was told he couldn't ride out come spring, why, he might start out even earlier: wasn't *nothing* on God's earth that was going to keep him off them trails to the villages and all them empty walls that needed reminders of what God expected of everbody. Anyways, the doc done what he could, rigging up a sling and a kind of harness for Galvez, which would keep him from moving his arm, and he made regular calls at Vigil's through the winter weeks. Meanwhile, Vigil found plenty of work for me, fixing up the casita for his son and new wife to move into.

Might have been mid-March when Doc Archer took the sling and harness off and said to Galvez he should move the arm around gentle to get some new blood going through there. Galvez didn't say nothing to this, and he didn't do nothing, neither, just left the arm hanging there, useless, while he did everthing with the right hand. He was naturally right-handed, and so there wasn't no real reason why he couldn't have taken up his pencils or his brushes and made drawings of one thing and another around the place, if just to get back into practice. Santa Fe was too big for him to have a hope of saving it with paintings of its churches, but yet he could have started in doing some work, if it was just a drawing of a dish or a glass. Instead, all he did was sit in the front parlor, which once had been part of the dance floor, smoking and looking out the window. It was April by now, and all them pretty fruit trees come into blossom and the air so sweet, but he didn't show no interest. A couple of times I asked would he like to have a stroll down to the square where there was benches under the trees and a fair number of old-timers down there, smoking and telling stories to each other, but he only shook his head no; just sat there and looked out. One day I come back with some materials for the casita, and I seen some scraps of paper near the chair he favored when he wasn't in his room. They was the beginnings of drawings of some buildings across the way, but, really, you had to squint hard to make out what them scratches was meant to be.

A man can get out of practice with anything he customarily does, whether throwing a rope or shoeing a horse, but he can get back into it, if he's a mind to. Here, it was plain to Vigil and me that Galvez had no interest in painting nor anything else if he couldn't go out to the villages and the churches. Not even talk. When you said something to him he might come back with a word or two but nothing more than that, and most times didn't answer at all. Mealtimes was awkward that way, though gradually Vigil and me got so we'd talk along and not try getting him to join in. Whoever he may be, you got to respect a feller's silence and not be poking and prodding him to flap his jaws just to make you comfortable. The last year or so of Frank's life was that way; 'sad' ain't the word for it: it was more like he was thinking real hard about something that was important to him and didn't want you to bother him while at it. Maybe Galvez, too, was thinking that way. If he was thinking back on his life, he had plenty of things to ponder, pardner, that's for certain.

One fine afternoon I got it into my head to see if I couldn't get him to doing something more than just sit by the window, and I got out the easel and other materials and set them up at the back of the house where I could keep an eye on him while I was smoothing out the floor of the casita before finishing it with ox blood. Over the south wall of Vigil's place was a long house; you could see the pitched roof and chimney and the upper part of the windows. But what made it interesting to look at was a big apricot tree that dropped some of its branches over the wall, and I thought it was so pretty just then that maybe it might catch Galvez's attention, enough to want to paint it, even if it wasn't a church. Well, he come out, looked at the easel and chair, and sat down. I went back to my work but hadn't been at it long when he called for me. 'Here,' he says, handing me the brush, 'make an outline of that house, and I'll fill in the rest.'

Of course, I didn't know what to do: I had handled his brushes plenty down through the years, setting them out, reshaping them, and so forth, but never had held one in a business-like way. I looked back at him sitting there solid in the chair, hoping he didn't really mean it, but he just nodded toward the next-door house and the tree, so there wasn't nothing to do but moisten the brush and dip it in the cake of black and commence to put it to the paper. It come out all wrong. The sizes of things was way off, with the chimney so big I didn't hardly have room for even the start of the roof. There weren't any room for the apricot, neither, which in a way would have been the point of the picture, so to say. I had just enough room at the bottom for the very top of the wall, so it was really just a picture of a monstrous chimney, but nothing more. I wish I had that picture now, as it was real comical. Not at that time, though.

'Your house needs more paper,' he says from behind. That kind of stung me, but yet it was the first spark from him since he fell off his mule, and in that way I was grateful. He had me tack up another sheet and try again, but it was no better, just a terrible mess that he couldn't have done nothing with, even if so minded, which he wasn't. That was the end of that trial, and while I was damn glad of it, I was sorry, too, that I had disappointed him. But the next day, I'll be goddamned if he didn't set up the easel himself, one-handed, and call me to it, just when I was looking forward to noon dinner. I done no better, and trying to fit the tree in way at the edge, I smeared the paint so that you couldn't make out that it was a tree—looked more like a cyclone had come down to roost in the neighbor's back space.

Next day, I was finishing the casita's floor and trying hard to come up with an excuse to go somewheres to get away from the humiliation at the easel, which Galvez didn't seem to notice, or if he did, he didn't care about it none. He had tacked up a fresh sheet, and now he had me start with the tree instead of the chimney. The tree was then so pretty it felt shameful to mess with it the way I was bound to. I had just made a few lines of it when he says, real sharp, 'You start too slow! *Ándele! Ándele!* Go! Go! Don't look down!' And, by Godfrey, working that way things begun to go a tad better, or so they seemed to me, anyways. Galvez didn't say nothing one way or another, but at least he was now taking an interest in *something*, and so I kept at it, just about ever day.

Then come an early evening when he had me at the easel again, and what I was producing was only a bit better than before, but now he says, 'Why are you using your left hand?' I told him I couldn't grip the brush proper with my right.

'Who told you so?' he asks. I said the Kid, way back at San Patricio when he was getting me started as a left-handed gunman. 'The Kid wasn't nothing but a killer,' he said, short-like. 'The only thing he knew was how to kill. Using your hand to kill is not the same as using it to paint. When you use your hand to kill, you are taking away something that can never come back. When you use that same hand on a fresh paper, you are making something that was not there before. Use the hand God gave you, not what your enemy gave.'

When I changed hands with the brush I swear it felt like I was trying to work with a tree trunk, and I was shaking my head when he come up quick from the chair and grabbed my hand with a grip like iron and pushed and pulled it along, *ándele*, and here comes the tree, snaking along over the wall and also what you could see of the side door and then the roofline and the chimney, set up there just proper, everthing perfectly clear, and the sizes just right for one another. Then he let go and sat back down while I was working my fingers that was practically stuck together from being held so hard. When I looked back at him, he had sort of caved in on himself and was just a feeble old man again.

*

That was my last lesson. After it, I didn't do no more work at the easel on account of Vigil got me a job breaking horses up in Tesuque, and I was away from the house all day. When I come back one evening he was waiting to tell me old Galvez was dead: Vigil had gone into his room with the morning coffee, and there was Galvez, with his hands folded on his chest, and Vigil knew at first look that he weren't asleep. Just never woke up. While he was telling me this, I was thinking of the way I had seen some others die—shot to death—and that this was the best way. Later on, of course, the sadness sunk in.

We went out back to talk about what to do next. Far as we knew, Galvez had no living kin, no money for a funeral, no home place where we might think to take the body. But Vigil had a family cemetery here in town and said he would see to the details, which he begun to do that same evening, getting a woodworker cousin to come to the house and knock together a coffin from some good heavy boards left over from the casita.

The cemetery was at the edge of town where the houses begun to thin out and there was some little farms and a goat rancher whose flock looked like they had eaten off part of the hillside. Next day, Vigil and me and the cousin went up past that in the wagon, and about halfway to the top we pulled up at the cemetery and got the box down and through the gate. The graves was scattered here and there, not set in rows as you might see in some other such places but situated close to junipers or piñons, almost like the kinfolks had in mind providing shade for their dead. There was as many Apodaca folks in there as Vigils, I noticed, but maybe the families was all one, some way. Then we got to work with the pick and shovels with the box laying there in the shade. The cousin had worked through the night to put it together, and he had done a fine job. The wood was sanded nice where you could see it, the corners was plumb, and the lid was snug and thick—an important consideration, as back in them days there was lean and hungry bears prowling about in springtime up there, and if they could smell something rotting under the earth, they might well try to tear down to it.

We had him laid out real simple. Neither Vigil nor me wanted to go buy him a new suit for the occasion, as Garrett was said to have done for the Kid. It wasn't that we judged he wasn't worth it, but as we had talked through it we concluded he should be put away like he had lived. He always traveled light in personal things: a big old frock coat, one skillet, a heavy Mex blanket that was considerable patched. The rest was his materials. We decided the frock coat would serve as his lay-out suit. I remember lifting him off his bed while Vigil struggled him into it, how *light* he felt, even with that head and them huge hands, and you'd have thought you'd have to really *go* some to lift him. But no: it was like lifting a whisper, if that don't sound too loco. Anyways, it's what come to me at that time. We buttoned it all the way to the chin, and he looked pretty lost in it, but then, if you was to allow yourself to go on in that way, thinking up improvements, why, you'd never get the feller buried, while not changing his condition none. So, that's the way we put old Galvez under, along with his materials, except for the easel and two fine-pointed brushes that I wanted as keepsakes. Vigil said some things in Mexican, sung a bit of a song, then quit, and we stood there in the sun and clouds, and only one bird singing somewhere close by, like a one-man choir.

On the way back to the wagon I noticed quite a few broken bottles which I hadn't seen on the way in. Of course, I didn't say nothing about these to Vigil nor the cousin, but I was wondering if they was left by family members who come out there to have a friendly drink in the company of their kin. Mexicans always seemed to me on better terms with the dead, whereas no white man I know would be caught getting drunked-up sitting atop a bunch of stiffs.

*

Back on Galisteo the three of us sat around in the kitchen where Vigil had put out a jug of mescal and three ironstone mugs.

Nasty stuff, mescal, like I said before, but at least this jug didn't have no dead worm in it, whereas in Old Mexico they do that for flavoring, they say. Once you get past the smell, it can go down okay if you're talking right along as we was, with Vigil and me saying neither one of us had a single scrap of paper with Galvez's work on it. All his work was up in the villages. Even that unfinished painting from Cañoncito had vanished somewheres; I wondered if maybe Galvez had destroyed it. Then we got on to the matter of a marker, which we judged he ought to have. We had the name, all right, at least we had the name he traveled under. Maybe it was the name he had when born, and maybe it wasn't, which would make him like so many them days. I never said a word to Vigil about Galvez's story. Maybe he knew it, but I doubt it. We also had a date, but only the one. Who knew how old he was?, maybe only Galvez when he come to the end of his trail here. Lacking these things, what we come up with was like what we settled on for his burial layout—real simple: JNG. That's the whole of it, nothing else. Next time you happen to be up in Santa Fe, if you was to find your way over to that cemetery, you could go to the grave and see for yourself. If you do, pardner, remember to take your goddamn hat off.

*

I almost wish that had been the end of that day, but it wasn't: you go through something like that, and then you sit around with a jug, talking through it, but as the jug gets lighter and lighter you find you're talking about everthing *except* what brung you to the table and the jug to begin with. Best to quit when the true occasion has been talked through, but that don't happen too often, and it didn't with us on Galisteo. By the time the cousin had heard enough and left, we was on to the history of the house and how it was once a dance hall. And that got Vigil going on the Kid who used to play monte in here, and, my, wasn't it something to see how popular he was with all the gals and was such a fine dancer: real light on his feet and knowing just how to swing them, not throwing them about like a farmer pitching hay bales. That was a lot of what went into his popularity, Vigil said, but soon as he said it, he wondered whether there wasn't something more to it than that.

'After all,' he says, 'he was quite a little feller, really, and had them forward teeth. The men that come in here used to wonder what it was about him, especially when the Kid would sail in and right away get the attentions of gals that had arrived with other dancing partners. That kind of thing can cause big trouble in a place like this, but it never happened where the Kid was concerned. The boys just had to kind of bite their lip, have another drink, and wait till the Kid had finished with their gal. Of course, it made a difference, him being who he was, even amongst them rough sorts that used to come in here, looking for a woman or a fight, whichever come first. But even those fellers didn't want to start nothing with little Billy. Somehow, Vigil said, shaking his head, he looked more dangerous out on the dance floor without his gun than any of those badmen with their irons hanging off them.

'Be damned if I can explain it, but it was so, anyways. Makes you wonder was the gals feeling something when they was close up to him in the dance—like they was in the arms of Death itself? Here they was, dancing with *Billy the Kid*, a man everbody knew had already killed many a man and was going to go on and kill many more before he got his time and somebody killed him. This dancing was just what he done in his spare moments, you might say. What he really done was kill. So, when a gal was dancing with him, maybe that's what she was feeling: that he was taking time off from his real work to dance with her, just this one time, and then he'd go back to his work. That would be a thrill she couldn't look to get no place else.'

I was having some trouble following Vigil here, as it was something of a ramble he'd taken, and I had been holding up my end of lifting the jug, making it extra hard to make sense of most things, let alone trying to think about a feller that smelled like death to the gal he's got his arms around. But then, of a sudden, Vigil pops up from the table and says to wait there a minute while he gets something from the other room he wants me to see. I could hear him in there, ransacking a desk or a bureau for that something, and then he comes back with a silver dollar and says to hold out my hand, which I done. It had a fair-sized bite taken out of its lower right edge, and Vigil said the Kid had won it in a shooting match over to Tascosa and had give it to him in here one night after he'd been cleaned out at monte, as this was all he had left.

'He had on that small smile,' Vigil said, 'when he handed it over; said he'd been carrying it a while as a good-luck piece. Said whenever he happened to reach inside his vest pocket and feel the ragged edge of it, it reminded him that he was still a good shot, even if, sometimes, his luck at monte wasn't so good.

"'I'd rather be good than lucky,"' he says to me with that little smile. "'Goodness you have ever day, where luck, you don't."'

*

Later that night I was shook wide awake with the feeling that someone was there in the room, standing real close in the dark. Scared hell out of me, but as I laid there, trying to puzzle it out, it come to me that wasn't nobody but me in there, and what had shook me so was the thought that right then was the first time in all my life that I had woke up without old Galvez being somewhere here on earth instead of under it, out on that hillside at the edge of town. I got up and went into his room and felt along the bed to see if there might be anything left of him there, maybe just a wrinkle or a dent, but there wasn't nothing but a

189

folded blanket that had nothing to do with him. Standing there for some minutes, I knew better than to try to go back to bed, though it was so black outside I figured it must be around two, which is just where the night is like taking a deep breath and means to hang on forever.

Out on Galisteo, I begun walking away from the plaza where there might be a light or three and a couple of drunks shoving one another around. I didn't want lights nor company just then nor sounds, neither, but my boots was making a real big noise in all that black quiet, so that I thought sure I must be waking folks and making them wonder who in hell was stomping around at such an hour, when even the roosters was still asleep. Sure enough, I roused some dog that was probably chained up behind a fence, and his woofs was deep enough to make me glad there was that fence between us. I went on, leaving him woofing at nothing, following the rise and fall of the road, walking a bit smarter now that I had the feel of how the road went, and feeling, too, that I was working through the last of all that mescal inside me.

A minute ago I was saying to you that I almost wished that day had ended after we'd dropped the last dirt on Galvez and right there had said all of what we had to say about him and left it at that. Instead of which, me and Vigil spent far more time going on about the Kid and the way he done. Why, I was wondering, was that? Why was I still doing it now, out in the dark by myself, when in reason I should have been thinking over what had brung me out on the road in the first place, the loss of Galvez?

That day when I was at the easel, Galvez had made a judgment on the Kid, when he said the Kid was nothing but pure killer that never made nothing, except dead men. I heard that, all right, but I really didn't pay much mind to it, as I was busy trying to figure out what to do with the god-awful mess I had made on the paper. And then Galvez followed that up by making me switch hands and grabbing my right hand, just like a vice and making it move quick along the paper. Now, though, clomping along the road, where the only light I seen was a lamp burning low and brownish in a window where someone had gone to bed without snuffing it, I come back in mind to that judgment. And then that brung to mind what Vigil said about what them dance hall gals might be getting when up close to the Kid, with the music going and him swinging them light and high: the smell of death—gunpowder, blood, and that peculiar odor a body gets when it's been out in the weather a while—, what I smelled when they brung Tunstall down to my place and unwrapped him from off the mule to put him in the wagon for Lincoln. Maybe, I thought, them gals wasn't the only ones to get that feeling—not the dancing and being swung, but the feeling of being close up to death. Why else am I sitting here this minute, telling you about that night on Galisteo and how terrible black it was when there's been many and many a deep black night for me: nights when I've laid awake in my bed and Cella next to me and her fair hair played out on the pillow in my direction, but me not being comforted none by that but instead thinking of them far-off days when I was in the company of the outlaw of all the outlaws that ever was, and ever moment around him felt like being close up to death? Maybe I'm not so different after all from the rest of you folks that still comes down here, poking around the graves over to Old Fort Sumner, trying to find the exact spot where the Kid went down, going over to Lincoln town, looking for old bullet holes or the ashes of McSween's house. It's all the Kid, the Kid, the Kid. And what is the Kid but what Galvez said? Maybe, in a way of thinking, I've kind of been dancing with Death all these years, but never would name it.

*

Well, there I was, yet clomping away steady, past the last of town and on my way to nowhere once again, like I was long

191

ago after leaving the Sugarite, the village of Galisteo being far off—walking in the blackness, wondering as I went what Galvez would've made of all this if he could see out from under that stout coffin and all the dirt and rocks we piled atop him. Here, he had tried to make a painter out of a feller that was maybe after all really more interested in his outlaw days and in the Kid than in making something new on paper or canvas. Galvez sure enough changed his life, making good things out of a terrible one. And I guess, you'd have to give me some kind of credit for having changed my own ways a bit. This was why that scripture from Matthew was his favorite, for it's about just that: changing your life. 'Whosoever will save his life shall lose it. Whosoever will lose his life for my sake, shall find it.'

As I say, I have puzzled over this a good deal down the years, as it looks like it runs contrary to good sense. I've asked others about it, them that knows the Bible well enough to be worth listening to. Also, some preachers, though only a few, as I have found many of them was ignorant and loco to boot, or only wanted to talk to you about spreading the good word. *Horseshit!* This scripture don't have a thing to do with spreading nothing. No, sir, what Matthew is up to here is talking about how *you* are going to live *your* life, not how another man will live his.

You start out when your pa or someone like him puts you up on a horse, slaps his rear, and away you go, hitting the trail that leads on. But some ways along there comes a fork, and there you got to make a choice. The left-hand fork looks broader, better traveled than the right. The man who takes that left-hand one, we'll say, is the man who wants to stay pretty much with the life he has, the one he knows about. He knows he done some bad things, has some bad habits, has maybe even done some crimes. But still, this is the life he knows, and that's what's the most important thing to him—just that comfort with his old ways. Whereas that other feller has done some bad things as well, sinned and so on. He don't know where that right-hand fork is leading, but he knows one big thing: he can be a better man than he has been up to that point, and so he takes that right fork, and he *keeps to it*, though maybe tempted again and again to double back to the left-hand one, which is well marked. The reason he keeps on the new way is that he has hopes it will lead him to a peaceable place, like a meadow with good water, whereas he knows the old trail likely will end him up in a box canyon, where there ain't no way out. The man who keeps to that left-hand fork thinks he is *saving* his life, don't you see, but is like to lose it in the end by continuing his old, bad ways. The other feller loses his old life but has the *chance*, anyway, of saving his soul by making a new life for himself.

Hendry. I thought of him then, how brave he was when we busted out of that burning shed, me scrunching along behind him, while he worked his rifle this way and that, and made some of our enemies think twice about raising up to fire on us. Thereafter, he took that right-hand road, become a lawman, was respected by his town. But somehow, it come to him to double back and get on the old road, the outlaw trail. Who knows why? Maybe he judged he was better suited to it after all. If that's what it was, I believe he badly misjudged his own character. There was a powerful amount of good to old Hendry.

There was good in the Kid, too. Many who knew him, like Frank and me, and Sallie Chisum and Governor Wallace seen that. Sure, it was mixed in with lots of other stuff that was black as two-in-the-morning. But that don't mean it wasn't there. I believe that when me and Frank was with him outside of Anton Chico, he was right where the trail forked for him, and knew it. He believed his chances was best by taking that left-hand fork where he could live by being so good with the gun. Luck comes and goes, sure enough, like he told Vigil, but not that quickness, that steadiness he had under all conditions. Well, as it happened, that didn't do him no good at last when luck run out, there being another man in that dark bedroom besides Pete Maxwell when the Kid come backing in, a man steady enough and good enough with a gun, and who knew that voice of old—.

Now I hear voices, myself. Must be Cella, and from the sound of it, she's got her sister along. Be a real pardner, will you? and put this here jar back up on that top shelf and roll that striped pot in front of it: Cella don't like to see it. Says it's too ghostly.

THE END

CPSIA information can be obtained
at www.ICGtesting.com
Printed in the USA
LVHW04s2321290618
582304LV00001B/74/P